JUDY LEE BURKE

BLACKROCK

A SUSPENSE THRILLER

Barringer Publishing, Naples, Florida
www.barringerpublishing.com
Cover, graphics, layout design by Lisa Camp
Editing by Jessica L. Delashmit

ISBN: 978-0-9908209-1-8

Library of Congress Cataloging-in-Publication Data
Blackrock / Judy Lee Burke

Printed in U.S.A.

THIS BOOK IS DEDICATED TO

Christine, Morgan and Evelyn Jones
Mark and Lauren Hackman-Brooks
Thomas J. Burke and L. Elaine Burke
Christine Villas-Boas and Robert S. Paskulovich

ACKNOWLEDGEMENTS

I am grateful to the following family, friends, students, writers, graphic artist, photographer, and editors for helping me shape my novel. Over the years, their encouragement and advice has inspired me. This book would not exist without their support and contributions. Thank you!

Dr. Christine M. Jones, Mark A. Brooks, Dr. Morgan Jones, Thomas Burke, L. Elaine Burke, Lt. Commander Robert S. Paskulovich, U S Navy, Elmore Leonard, Elizabeth Kane Buzelli, Jean Harrington, Wilfrid Burke, Christine Villas-Boas, Claire Gudefin, Dr. Linda Carrick, Michael Kiefer, Calvin Khemmoro, Nancy Young, Maggie Mc Clellan, Deborah Newcomer, Dorta Kosa, John Nelson, Ken Prather, Judith Searle, Geraldine Hemple Davis, Sara Reeside, Patricia Currence, Ann Waldt, Abigail Stonerook, Tom Klieber, Elizabeth Klieber, Hanna Lore, Elizabeth Stillwell, Phyllis Reeve, Mark Reeve, Margie Reins Smith, Nancy Solak, Marlene Harle, Wilma Montel, Dianne Peters Pegg, John Minnis, Dr. Bonnie Ellis, Marureen O'Halleran, Darrett Pullins, Kevin Walsh, Cynthia Keleman, ADM William J. Fallan, U S Navy, CAP Terrance Bronson, U S Navy, Zach Ogden USCGMB3, Captain USAR Alan Anderson, Rev. Peter Donohue, OSA, Robert Capone, Robert O' Neil.

Honorable mention goes to my children Christine and Mark, my editors and readers, who have shared ideas and given me inspiration and support. Their editing and advice, both personally and professionally, have made the novel what it is today. To my parents, Tom and Elaine, who

BLACKROCK

gave me the opportunity, education, and incentive to pursue my writing career. And for that, I am forever grateful. To my friend Robert who has encouraged me to write, and has provided me with a positive atmosphere to keep me writing. I thank you many times over. To my cousin, Christine, I give thanks for sunshine in the darkest days of my writing and lending new insights into my characters' lives. To Nancy Young who has read all my revisions and persevered until the end, thank you. To Geraldine Hempel Davis who encouraged me to publish my work—cheers to you Driving Diva. I want to say a special thanks to my *Writer's Group* and my friend Phyllis Reeve. It was her enthusiasm that kept me on track in tumultuous times. I cannot thank you enough. To Elmore Leonard, who helped me endlessly with the writing of the first draft through the last draft. His inspiration and encouragement drove me to my best efforts in writing the novel. I cannot be more grateful to have such a patient and encouraging mentor. To Elizabeth Kane Buzelli, Brenda Hiatt, Cynthia Harrison, and Jean Harrington who have inspired me and provoked my thoughts to make me a better writer. Your conversations and suggestions encouraged me to move to higher levels in my writing—thank you. Also, to Judith Searle who reminded me to examine the 'beat' in my character's dialogue—it has given life to my characters. To Maggie McClellan who has helped me to paint my scenes on canvas while the writing flowed on paper. Also, to Chuck Sambuchino, who inspired my creative thoughts and ideas. To Kenneth Prather and John Von Ophem, who helped me pull it all together, thank you. To Matthew Klug, my technical advisor, who kept me up to date, many thanks. To Jeff Schlesinger, my publisher, who has given me the opportunity to publish the novel, after years of hard work writing it. Finally to my editor Jessica Delashmit, your attention to detail has helped me with the revisions and moved the story along. I am forever grateful to all of you.

CÉAD MÍLE FÁILTE
(A HUNDRED THOUSAND WELCOMES)

ONE
BLACKROCK ISLAND
IRELAND

The white glow from the Bell Jet Ranger strobe lights pierced the darkness. The blonde woman slid into the pilot's seat, fastening the harness. Holding in the starter button, she engaged the helicopter's generator, slowly releasing it. After a minute, flipping switches on the instrument panel, she stared at the green lights illuminating the cockpit and completed the start sequence.

Placing her hands on the controls, she forced them into position. The whirling blades beat the air as the turbine whined to a high pitch for takeoff. The rotors thumped as the skids bounced on and off the landing circle, dirt flying. The dim light of the cockpit was silhouetted against the dark forest.

In one swift motion, the Irish peacekeeper's fist punched upward at a forward angle. "Halt!" He shouted, gripping the bullhorn with his other hand.

The woman stared directly at him from the cockpit. The skids scraped the tarmac as the helicopter lifted off.

"Prepare to fire on my command!" His troops lined up for the kill shot.

Kneeling, facing forward, weapons at the ready, men clad in black steadied their fifty caliber sniper rifles into their shoulders.

"Fire!"

A barrage of bullets riddled the target. The helicopter exploded, sending shards of metal in all directions as the bright orange flames scorched the black sky.

TWO
A WEEK EARLIER
MANHATTAN, NEW YORK

Laine Sullivan stared at the caller ID as the cell phone vibrated on the antique French desk. Outside her window, Central Park hummed with activity. She shoved the stack of architectural designs aside and logged into her laptop. She stashed the picture of her late husband John inside her desk drawer.

"Hello, Max," she said softly into the phone. "Haven't talked to you since John's accident." She pushed the speakerphone button and grabbed her pen on top of the classified document.

"Thanks for taking the call."

"You knew I would." The computer screen filled with images. Max's call was nothing but bad news. She had a year's worth of bad news since

John's accident—she wanted her life before she got married, but that wasn't going to happen. This is the part that caught in her throat, shoving down what she really wanted to say to Max. Shoulders tight, eyes alert yet not seeing, she remembered the last assignment Max had sent her on. Smoke in her lungs, breath rushing out, cold, hard metal on her back as she was airlifted out. He'd make light of it, so she said nothing, staring at the laptop.

"You've read the file?" The man's voice from headquarters was hard, professional.

"Yes, but you already know that." She waited, watching the flurry of information flood her screen.

"I do," he said in a hard tone. "Got the written updates?"

"Yes." A photo of a man in a tailored suit filled her screen. A jockey stood close to him, engaged in conversation. They were pointing at a dark horse fitted for a race. She flipped open the document folder and gazed at the same photo inside—handsome, she thought. He wasn't too bad looking for a blonde—not really her type.

Max said, "That's Miles Bourke, thirty-five-year-old bachelor, privately educated, and one of the wealthiest thoroughbred racehorse and stud farm owners in Ireland and France."

"Young for all that," she said. Another image of him at a farm with thoroughbred horses filled her screen. She loved horses. Max knew it.

"He is as privileged as they come. The man to his right is his jockey at Lucre—his private racetrack in Blacksod on the west coast of Ireland."

"Well, fancy that—good looking horses, too."

"The one ready for the race is the multimillion-dollar winner Midnight Madness."

Fans in the background were waving programs and pointing at the horses on the track.

"Quite the state-of-the-art racetrack. Who builds something like that along a seashore?"

"Like I said—lots of money in the Bank of Ireland—a Euro billionaire. His buyers include sheiks, princes, international breeders, U.S. 'big boys'—you name it. But… it's more involved than that. That's why I called you."

"It can't be good. I told you I retired from all this." She stared at the horse, the man, and the racetrack.

"We've got a situation. I need you for an undercover operation in Ireland."

"I'm not in that kind of business anymore—not since my husband's death."

"I know, but you were never discharged. And you owe me," he said in a firm tone.

"I know that, but I'm not ready. I don't know if I'll ever be ready again."

"You haven't been out that long—you're a natural. I need you to gather intel on money laundering and drug trading at the racetrack overseas. It's simply gathering the information and reporting back to me."

"Not a chance," Laine said, and hung up.

THREE
MANHATTAN

The phone rang and rang. Laine finally picked up. "No, Max, what about 'no' don't you understand?"

"Take a look at your laptop," he said in a gentle tone.

"Oh no!" she said in a loud voice.

A sleek brown thoroughbred racehorse was sprawled on its side on the racetrack—black, dead eyes staring out at her, white foam seeping from its nose and dripping onto the dirt. Its back knees were buckled under its belly while the front legs jutted out at odd angles. A jockey was dressed in full bright colors. Dirty cheeks were streaked with tears as he knelt near the horse's head, rubbing his neck.

"The official verdict is 'milkshaking.'"

"What's that?"

"An energy boost injected through the horse's nostril before the race.

Supposed to make them run faster."

"Like athletes on steroids?"

"Yes, but the effects are lethal."

"What kind of psycho would do that to a horse?" She saw the veins popping out on the horse's neck. Horrified, she scrolled down, removing the scene from her view.

"We don't know, but we want to find out. Horse was running in first place at the Kentucky Derby, until this happened. Never made the finish line and dropped dead in front of all the fans. Saudi Arabian Sheik Abdullah had a lot of money riding on that beauty. Bourke sold it to him, but he said he had no part in the injections. They are illegal."

"Someone wanted revenge. What else do you have?"

"Nothing. That's where you come in."

"Go on." She focused on the next photo of Miles angry, shouting at a man.

Max was silent, paper rustling in the background. "Hold on."

She pulled out a pen and made notes. Maimed horses—she didn't know if she had the stomach for it. She attended charity events to protect horses and keep them safe from harm. This was sickening and too much to imagine.

She loved horses her whole life and even had a few. She couldn't stand any animal abuse. Max knew he had her with that photo videos—damn him. What was he doing?

"I said 'go on,'" she told him in a loud voice.

"Here it is. The update says same thing happened at the *Abu Dhabi Irish Guinness Festival*. It's an Arabian village atmosphere during race days. The Irish and the Emirati come together—over money, that is. A lot of money changes hands—a lot more than we've been led to believe. That horse really suffered."

"I bet it did."

"Here is where you come in—where NOVAS comes in. Since you've been gone, we now operate under contract for a private agency, National Operations Venture Advancement Systems."

"A new title, but the same business?"

"Yes."

"And?"

"There was another milkshaking incident in Ireland. Bourke's horse was running in the *United Arab Emirates Cup* there.

"What happened?"

"His purebred Arabian horse stumbled to its knees, throwing the rider over his head in the last leg of the race. Horse was sweating and lathered behind the saddle, foam oozing out of its mouth. It buckled to the ground and rolled over, just as the jockey cleared his leg from under him."

She waited for him to continue, frowning.

"They shot him on the track in front of the crowd—same as the other incident. The racing committee was shocked. Fans were sickened. The Sheik Abdulla was beyond furious and wants revenge."

He liked telling it so much he ran his words together at mock speed.

"What can we do?" she said. "What do you want *me* to do?"

"NOVAS accepted the contract—unofficially. That's where you come in."

"Why is that?" she said in a clipped tone. She slipped a loose dark hair behind her ear. "Like I said, I'm not ready."

Laine looked at the other photos—the animal abuse lingering in her mind. Bourke, in jeans and a flannel shirt, was leaning against a wooden fence surrounding the racetrack. Behind him, horses ran along the dirt track, jockeys tight in their saddle. Off the track near the white stables, men flicking stopwatches shouted at the riders to speed up their time.

"You know the drill."

"I'm out of training."

"You're fine. We want you at Bourke's lighthouse on a remote island not

14

far from the Irish mainland. It's fifteen minutes flying time from Blacksod. That's where you'll be staying and getting information for us."

"No. I'm not going to take any more assignments." Again, the injured horse loomed in her mind. She felt compelled to help, but what could she do? She hadn't been in the field in months.

He ignored her and went on. "It's the meeting place for buying the horses."

A new photo popped up. "Who is the elderly couple on my screen?" They stood in front of a thatched-roof cottage.

"Bourke's seventy-year-old caretakers Eamon and his wife Patricia. They live in the lighthouse cottage on the island."

"It's isolated. What do you want from me, Max? You know I have a weak spot for horses." She remembered the old life, and she wanted it locked away. In New York she could do that—hide from her feelings.

From the aerial view she saw thick forests trailing along the black rock cliffs behind the cottage. The Atlantic was a rough, choppy sea of green surrounding the island. The cottage, lighthouse, and a helicopter pad were situated near the northwest forested area near the cliffs.

"I want you to get intel. You'll be undercover. Bourke knows you are an architectural designer, so it's perfect. Get information on what's going on with him and the horse racing. How you get it is up to you." His voice was hard. "We got Bourke's confirmation today. He hired you to redesign his party room in the lighthouse tower on Blackrock Island."

"No, Max."

"It's time."

"What are you talking about?" Laine said in an angry voice. "In case you've forgotten, I've been out of the business for over a year, since John's accident."

"Call it what you want, but it was not an accident."

FOUR

"It was an accident, Max. My husband knew Lake St. Clair and sailed it every summer."

Laine remembered sailing and her first impression of John Rafferty at the charity event in New York. Rebounding from her parents' deaths a few months earlier, she was a lonely target—not herself—the covert operative, but a needy woman in search of love. John was dressed in black tie, a triple-starched white dress shirt, sporting a red-striped bow tie. She liked what she saw. Long, dark hair curling over the collar of his jacket framed a suntanned face and dreamy blue eyes. Instead of sipping champagne, he drank Scotch. During the bidding, Laine went back and forth with him, bidding on an expensive lithograph until she won it. He congratulated her on her buy, smooth talking like she liked it. Smiling, he offered to take her to dinner. She went, but paid the bill when he discovered his wallet was missing.

Max was waiting. Giving her time to think.

"That's another story for another day. To update you on this operation, we are now a private company contracted by the U.S. government to get rid of special problems. This is one of those problems. John was another."

"What are you talking about??"

"Your boat was on the rocks. It was no accident—and we didn't find a body," he said, again in a hard voice. "Your husband planned it."

"You're wrong. He wouldn't do that to me. He had everything he ever wanted." Or did he, she wondered, thinking back. He had conned her down the aisle six months after they met. His easy manner and carefree style were deceptive—the actor—always on. In the beginning he was a lot of fun, but what a surprise to find out on their honeymoon he had no job—zero in savings. He told her he had his identity stolen, and he was working it out. He was living in a friend's place while he was looking for a new condo before they met. It was all a ruse. Later, she found out there was no condominium. She confronted him, but he had a million excuses and a lot of unpaid bills.

"The Border Patrol combed Lake St. Clair for over a month," he said and paused, "Like I said there was no body—no trace of any foul play. Nothing. They did everything they could to find him. Even NOVAS came up empty-handed. We combed the area for over a week right after it happened. I never told you because I wanted you to put it behind you."

"I didn't know."

"No. You wouldn't have. Your sailboat was smashed to pieces on the rocks in the South Channel. It was near Squirrel Island within the Canadian border when we examined it. We sent in divers and used head sensors with our planes from Selfridge Air Force base looking for clues. No John—no trace of him or anything else for that matter."

"Nothing, Max? He was the best solo sailor in Michigan. We never sailed there. Too shallow—he knew that."

"Nothing. There's a cover-up and your husband is part of it. It's all in the brief."

"I know you mean well, Max. We go back a long time," she said softly. "I'm trying to wrap my mind around it. Really, I am."

"It's the perfect opportunity to do something you're good at," he said.

"I know," she said. "If I'd only been sailing with John none of this would have happened." She didn't want to think of it anymore, but it haunted her. Kept her up at night—seeing his face in her dreams.

"You don't know that. He didn't tell you what was going on half the time. He was a con artist. Womanizing, gambling, drinking, running through your money—"

"Yes," she said. "I had some idea, but not to the extent it was going on."

"So, now you know. He's gone. Let go."

"Sure." She stared outside. Droplets of water slid down her window making trails on the glass.

Max was saying now, "You've got to move on. This job—this operation—is perfect for you."

She had stopped grieving months ago. It was over, but she still needed to know the truth.

"Maybe this assignment will help you put closure on things. There was no reason for your boat to be where it was—except for using it as a drug drop. The Coast Guard confirmed that's the drop-off point for all the drugs coming into the United States and Canada. Did he ever mention anything about drugs?"

"No, never," she said in a hard tone. "This is the first I've heard about it."

"Did you ever suspect he took drugs or sold them?"

"That would be a stretch even for him. Womanizing and drinking—yes. He was a conniving and convincing hustler—but drug dealer? Definitely no." But... what if she was wrong?

"I had to ask," he said in a low voice. "I know it's hard. The things we don't want to accept are hard to know."

"It's the nothingness that's hard to know."

"You really don't have a choice on accepting this assignment, you know."

"I have a choice."

"You were handpicked for this job. There's no option."

"I doubt it."

"You were. This goes higher than me—you fit the profile. I'm briefing you on the record. Just listen."

"Sure." She wondered about John.

"The lighthouse is Bourke's secondary residence. He owns a vast estate and a massive farm along the west coast in County Mayo. Got a slew of expensive thoroughbred racehorses from Blacksod to Donegal. It's the perfect setup for money laundering and drug dealing."

"Go on." She tried imagining the operation and being in Ireland—not so bad, if she didn't have a choice. Max was irritating, but he always had her best interests in mind. She could talk to him because they were close. She admired his work and his advice—but John planning his own death, dealing drugs—this was too much for her. It was a new twist.

He interrupted her thoughts. "The slide shows an aerial view of Bourke's farm, Lucre. You can see the layout of the stables and the racecourse. We've got close-ups of the interior of the stables in the next few slides."

"I see them."

"He flies himself back and forth to the island in his helicopter."

"Nice life." One she didn't have.

A helicopter popped into her view. Behind Bourke's frame was a sleek black Bell Jet Ranger 450. To the right of it, several barns sparkled white under red, shingled roofs. Stonewall fences penned in hundreds of grazing thoroughbred horses.

"Why me? You've got other operatives that can handle this."

"He's a bachelor. If anyone can gain his confidence, it's you. You can design the plans for his party room in the lighthouse. Get close to him, and find out what's going on behind the scene."

"What kind of trouble is he in?"

"He might have misappropriated funds. Could have skimmed off the top when he sold his horses, but we don't think so—someone did, and we have to find out who. A lot is at stake. In particular, the Saudi Arabian Sheik Abdulla, his wealthiest customer, is butting heads with him over this. Making all sorts of accusations."

"He has a death wish then," she said studying Bourke's angular jaw, chiseled cheekbones—a Marlborough cowboy type with an attitude.

She had been around plenty of those and avoided them. That was what made her husband John different—or so she had thought.

"We also discovered an American concern or unknown person or persons interfering in the brokering of Bourke's horse sales. The numbers are not adding up. We're trying to uncover a paper trail, but we are coming up empty-handed. Whoever did this was good at it."

"Right. They usually are. Let the CIA or FBI do their job," she said in a cold voice.

"NOVAS took the contract. U.S. business relations with Saudi Arabia are of paramount importance in the political scheme of things—"

"The horse racing business is a good place for a cover-up."

"We have a source there already, but they have not had any success. NOVAS is conducting 'research' in that part of the Atlantic. The project is to protect marine sanctuaries on the west coast of Ireland—especially for the whales off County Mayo. The President of Ireland knows we are there. She'll give us whatever help we need. But again, we're not operating in an official capacity on the other issues."

"I see." She focused on an aerial view of several men with Bourke seated in the stern of a ninety-foot wooden Trumpy yacht. She refurbished one in the Florida Keys.

"You can do this."

"Yeah right. Murdered horses, sheiks, drugs, DEA, money laundering, Saudi princes, Ireland—the whole works. Risky, if you ask me. Who is my backup over there?"

"No one," he said. "You will be on your own."

FIVE

"You drive a hard bargain, Max," Laine said.

"Bourke is going to pay you a lot of money to design a party room in his lighthouse tower. It's a double-dip. He entertains heavy hitters—breeders, racehorse owners. It'll be easy for you. You know the type."

"Yes, unfortunately I do know the 'type.' What about my investment in this new business of yours?"

"Already taken care of. You're on the payroll."

"Pretty confident aren't you?" She tucked the hair behind her ear, smiling. Her headache was fading.

"Have to be," he said.

"So what's the time frame?"

"Now—your own op. Thought you'd never ask."

"Great. Just great," she laughed. She heard the smile in his voice when he answered her. She'd never hear the end of it if she didn't take the job.

He'd act indifferent. Keep asking her until she gave in.

She pulled her 9mm Glock out of her desk drawer. She slid out the clip, loaded it, and snapped it back into place in less than thirty seconds. She set the safety, making up her mind. He'd wear her down eventually with incessant phone calls and reminders of the past. She hated knowing he had this effect on her.

"Here's the direction you can start with. Bourke owns several boats. The Trumpy impresses the big shots when he takes them to his island. Get on it. We believe he makes the most profitable sales on it or in his lighthouse. We can't confirm it, but I think you'll be able to find out."

"What do I have to do?" She slipped the pistol in her purse. If there was one thing she was good at, it was her talent for hitting the target. She was a top marksman and enjoyed practicing every week regardless of her time away from ops training. She walked into the front hallway and pulled out her Louis Vuitton suitcase.

"The car is scheduled to pick you up in half an hour. You leave from La Guardia and land in Donegal, Ireland tomorrow morning. We've got everything in place."

"What exactly is the mission called?" She carried the case into her bedroom and placed it on the bed. Walking over to her closet, she pulled out her black high heels and her black Chanel business suit. Next, she pulled out slacks, skinny jeans, sweaters, blouses, and undergarments.

"Labrador."

"Who is my contact?" She grabbed the pearl necklace and earrings from her jewelry box, putting them on.

"I am. You'll brief me every couple of days."

"That's different. How do I make contact with you? I've always had a handler."

"This is different, but use the same procedure—secure cell phone. Wait for my call. If something comes up, you'll have my number programmed into the phone. It's number seven on the speed dial. It will connect you directly to me 24/7."

"Things have changed."

"You will have everything you need when you land. If you need something else—just ask. We have an older man in Ireland who will bring what you need. You can't miss him because he is a town fixture. He herds his sheep to market once a week. Other times he drives his beat up old Ford truck into Donegal to pick up messages or tip a pint at Donahue's Pub. Name's Shamus."

"Sounds like a character," she laughed.

"He is. He knows everyone. We told him you'll be with Bourke starting tomorrow on his island."

"Tomorrow! How will he know me?"

"He'll signal you by taking his cap off, hitting it twice on his knee to knock off the dust, and placing it back on his head. NOVAS sent him your photo. You'll have his photo on your phone. Delete it after you look at it. His number is one if you need it in an emergency. He tips a few Guinness with the men at Bourke's farm so be on the lookout for him there, too."

"This is starting to sound like last time. That bomb in the Canadian Embassy in Cuba almost killed me."

"You survived didn't you?" He laughed.

"Thanks to your timely maneuver and the extraction team. Make it worth my while."

"Already did. I tripled your fee. It's being wired into your Swiss account as we speak. Plus Bourke is paying top dollar for your expertise."

"I see," she smiled. "You know how to charm a girl. Any new toys?"

"Absolutely, Techno has a kit for you. Show your gun at the airport. They will clear you. Also, check your luggage in the false bottom after you land. Everything you need will be there."

"I guess that's it," she said. "Anything else?" The rain left beaded trails of water zigzagging down the glass on her bedroom window.

"Bourke's the key. You're going to do whatever it takes to find out what he knows."

"Yes, whatever it takes." She sprayed herself with Coco Chanel and stashed it between her clothes in the suitcase.

"One last thing."

"Here it comes," she said, looking at her reflection in the mirror. Dark circles under her eyes reminded her of sleepless nights.

"He sells the horses to the Saudis and lots of other owners. Several million is missing from his last horse sale, but we don't know where it went—gun running, illegal drugs, mercenaries. Who knows? Looks like some of the races were fixed. Something out of Mexico, but we don't have a handle on it."

"Oh, so there is more," she said.

"You got it. There's an extremely expensive racehorse in line for the *Triple Crown*. There's a dossier in the suitcase. For now, find out what you can. Follow the money."

"Yeah, yeah, yeah, I know the drill." She finished the last of her packing and grabbed her passport.

"I know you do. Bourke is clean. We've had him followed, but someone wants us to think it's him. We have to find out who is running the scam. My guess is an amateur but smart enough to put us off the trail."

"No bombs this time?" She looked in the mirror and released her long hair, brushing the dark strands into place.

"No. You have my word on it. Locate the source that's putting our operation in jeopardy. Report intel only to me."

"Find the target. Socialize. No bombs. Okay." She swiped clear gel across her mouth and rubbed her lips together. "Contact Shamus in an emergency."

"Yes—that's all you have to do—easy assignment. Report back to me every couple of days. Or I will contact you."

"Yeah, sure. Same handle?"

"You got it. *Yellowbird.* Same everything," Max said. "And, you'll get to see where your ancestors were born."

"I knew you had an angle," she said and laughed. "I see you've done your homework. I should have known."

"When haven't I?" he said. "Are you in?"

SIX

Laine said in a strong voice, "When could I ever refuse you?"

"Good, I knew you'd see it my way," he said. "You have an hour. Talk to you tomorrow night."

"Sure," she said. She hung up, shaking her hair free. She turned down the air conditioner in the living room, closed the blinds, and set the security timer.

In her bedroom, she pulled several designer gowns from her closet and chose one.

"This'll do." She put the tight fitting black Ralph Lauren cocktail dress in the case, along with the rest of her garments, and zipped it shut.

Walking through her studio she wondered how she played that. If she was into aerobics, she'd say it was great, but she didn't exercise regularly. What was she trying to do talking to Max the way she did? It was probably a good idea to exercise her mind. Stay focused on the assignment. She was on her way to a new beginning, but beginning what she wasn't sure. She grabbed her classified papers, stuffing them into the Michael Khors designer portfolio. She placed the iPad mini and Kindle in her handbag, next to her weapon.

Closing the shades on her bedroom window shut out the light from the street. There was a loud knock on the door.

"Coming," she said. This better be good. She ran to the kitchen, grabbed her favorite *Earl Grey* tea in the small tin and slipped it into her carry-on. At least I can practice my interior design skills in another country, she thought.

On her way out the door, she snatched the picture of her husband from the table and dropped it into the trash bin along with her wedding ring. The door slammed behind her as the man in the dark suit took her bags and handed her a cell phone.

SEVEN
DONEGAL TOWN, IRELAND

Laine Sullivan and Miles Bourke sped out of Donegal airport in his convertible Mercedes Benz. In a short time, they bounced over the cobblestone streets of Donegal Town. As they passed the stone fountain in the center of the square, water flowed from the top over the edge of the second tiered bowl to the lower basin, and splashed onto the street. Water pooled at the base and seeped into the cracks. People walked along the sidewalks, stopping to peer into shop windows.

"I read about the boat you redesigned in *Architectural Digest*. I'd like to do my own."

"We can look at it," she said. You're talking about the Trumpy—not the fishing boat, correct?" She wondered if he really liked it or was trying to impress her.

"Yes." Miles steered toward the end of town passing the harbor. "Good fishing in this part of Ireland."

"I like fishing." She noticed the charter boats lined up along the docks. Max probably sent Bourke the yacht write-up, but he forgot to tell her the details. It bothered her. The little details could blow her cover.

"We'll pick a day and go out salmon fishing."

"I'd like that," she said, studying the layout of the town. All she had to do was look, and she could memorize it. It was the one thing she still had going for her.

He steered past the colorful blue and white awning of Donahue's Pub and outdoor deck.

"They cook fresh catch there. A drink and the harbor view is something you might enjoy later in the week."

"I'd like that," she said. "Speaking of fishing. We have fresh water salmon in Michigan."

"Never had it," he said, navigating the car through the crowds crossing the street.

"I see," she smiled, her voice in a friendly tone. She was warming up to him. "I've been toying with the design of the window in the lighthouse. We need to increase the size."

"Good idea," he said as they drove to the end of town near the church. "We're passing St. Patrick's on your right—tourists flock from all over to see the architecture." He motioned as they drove past. The Sunday bells chimed one o'clock as people exited the main doors.

"Legend says Christ showed St. Patrick an entrance to hell on that very spot, before the church was built."

"Oh, my God!" Laine said. "It can't be."

"That it is," said Miles. He pushed the pedal to the floor, and they took the turn heading out of town.

"No, I mean. Oh, Miles, stop the car! Stop. Please stop."

He braked and pulled off the narrow road. "What's the matter?"

"This is crazy, but I think I saw my husband in front of the church."

Miles stared at her. "Your husband?"

"Yes, I think he saw me too." She spun partway around in the seat, but the seatbelt stopped her. The road behind them twisted, blocking her view.

"I'm not sure I understand."

"No, you wouldn't. How could you?"

"Want to talk about it?"

"I thought I saw my husband with a woman. It gave me a shock."

"I'm sure it did," he said, shoving blonde hair from his forehead. "Want to go back?"

"No, Miles, no. Definitely, no." Creases lined her forehead. She stared at the farms flanking either side of the road. Tall hedges and low stone, walls surrounded hundreds of sheep marked with blue and red stripes grazing within the enclosures. It was a trick she learned on the job—focus on something else then make a decision. She had to pull herself together or he would think she was crazy. "I must be mistaken."

"I'm listening."

"I'm not sure how to begin, so I'll just say it. John, my husband, died in a boating accident in Michigan—a year ago." She felt her muscles tense. She was on full alert and her training kicked in. She told herself to remain calm and modulate her voice.

"I'm sorry for your loss."

"Thank you. It doesn't make sense that I think I saw him."

"It is puzzling. Let's go back and take a look. Maybe the man you saw resembled your husband." He said it in a nice way as if he cared about her.

"You're probably right. I may have mixed him up with someone else." She saw the man in her mind.

"No worries. We can be back in town in a few minutes."

"No, I have to be imagining it. Let's go on. Like you said, he resembled him—that's all. He's been gone a year." She wondered why he was in

Donegal, if that was him. Miles was looking at her, expecting something.

"Mind telling me what happened?"

"I don't really know."

Now coming down the road, a farmer and a young boy herding sheep approached the car. An elderly sheephearder tipped his tweed cap, removed it, and rapped his knee twice. He smiled at them while his walking stick tapped the road. A feisty dog raced along side the animals, barking and herding the sheep in place. "Miles," he shouted. "Good day to you and the misses."

"Shamus, to you, too."

They were under the shadow of the trees as the mass passed them. "If you want to talk, I'm a good listener."

"It's hard to tell." She nodded to Shamus.

She watched Miles watching her, interested in what she had to say. She could gain his trust and get something from him in return. Max's voice echoed in her mind—"Get the intel." This was a calculated guess on her part, but she'd give it a try. The memories sickened her.

He waited.

"My husband John disappeared after a sail boating accident near Squirrel Island— a channel off Lake St. Clair. The hull was smashed to pieces on the shallow rocks. No body. No life jacket. No wallet, money, or clothes. Not even keys. That's what's so strange to me. The Border Patrol in our area ruled out foul play."

Miles listened, as she told the story. "But you don't?"

"I don't know. He sailed alone a lot. There was no sign of a struggle or any proof he had been there, but he told me he was going solo sailing that week."

She wondered if she had given too much information by the way he looked at her—caring, compassionate. She was not used to anyone like that.

"Does seem strange," he said in a gentle voice.

"Maybe he got knocked in the head with the boom—fell overboard and got caught in the current. It could carry him all the way to Detroit and no one would ever know."

"Hard to say," he said.

"The officials gave up the search. So did I."

"Sorry for your loss." Miles said in a kind voice.

"Thank you. It's hard to lose someone you love. We were only married for a year. It still hurts to think about it."

"Yes," he said.

"I didn't really know him like I thought I did—seems I didn't know him at all," she said in a hard tone. She saw him flinch and said in a soft voice, "There's no resolution."

"It's hard to know someone," Miles said.

"Yes, especially since we lived in different cities. I worked in my studio in New York. Flying back and forth to our home in Grosse Pointe wasn't ideal."

"Sounds like you had separate lives."

"I was busy with work. When I had work off, he wanted to party with everyone all the time—big drinker. Not my kind of life."

"It can be a curse," Miles said. "The drinking, that is."

"Terrible. I asked him for a divorce a few days before he went missing."

"How did he take it?"

"Don't think he really cared. Partied, and drank more Scotch at the club."

"Not a nice man," Miles voice was hard.

"It had been over for a long time. But drowning—I wouldn't wish that on anyone."

"Loss from a death is permanent. It's the one thing we can't take back."

"I never saw him again after that last conversation," she was comfortable telling him. "I thought taking this job would help me forget the past, but when I saw that man in town, it all came back to me. Sorry to burden you." She wanted to win him over even if it was the truth. This was something new to her—she was not used to the feeling.

"Sometimes we need to get it out. The bad things that are making us sick."

"Yes, the bad things seem to take up all the space," she said.

"Aye, that they do."

They sat for a few minutes in silence.

Miles said, "Change of view may take your mind off things."

"Good, I could do with a change."

Dark, thick clouds hovered in the west. She kept her eyes on the trees bending under the wind, scraggly and broken in parts.

"I've got a Bell Jet Ranger-407—safest helicopter made, waiting for us."

He started the car and headed for the helicopter landing pad.

EIGHT

In a short time, Miles swerved into the parking lot near the helicopter launching zone. "About twenty minutes flying time in this wind."

Laine's eyes widened. "We're not taking *that!*"

"We are," he laughed.

"It's gorgeous." She liked the sleek black body of the copter—first class design.

"That it is."

"Let's go," she said, climbing out of the car. "You're sure you know what you're doing?"

"Absolutely. A few of us from town took lessons years ago. Wilfrid, Marla, Shamus—some learned more than the others." He laughed. She could see he remembered something.

"Logged in a thousand hours of flight time," he said, leading her to the aircraft and she climbed aboard. "I've got it handled."

"If you say so."

"Patricia and Eamon, my caretakers, will have dinner for us on the island. They practically raised me like second parents."

"I'm looking forward to meeting them." She wanted to ask him about the town people, but a bolt of lightening lit the sky.

"Not good," he said looking west.

"No," she said, fastening the harness and pulling on her headset. "All set."

"We're off," he said after checking the controls. In a few minutes, they left the tarmac and flew over the Atlantic, heading toward the island.

As they swept through the sky, Laine thought about the man who had smiled at her in front of the church. She knew it was John.

NINE
DONEGAL TOWN SQUARE

"What the hell, Marla, I saw *her*," John said. *"My wife, Laine!* What's she doing in Donegal?" He ran his hand through his dark, wavy hair. "Give me a cigarette. Maybe she knows I'm alive." He lit it, drew a deep breath, and sent out a smoke ring. "This is the worst. I can't believe it."

"You're imagining things," Marla said, high heels clicking as they walked down the street to his old Ford truck. "You read your own obituary to me, Johnny—*John Rafferty*—died on... or whatever it said. She had a memorial for you, didn't she? Good thing you changed your name to Jack Lafferty."

"She's a lot smarter than you think, Marla." He rubbed his chin, looking at the place where the car went by him with her in it. "I know her." He inhaled and blew another ring.

"So what if she is smart?" Marla said giving him a peck on the cheek.

"We can take care of that."

"What do you mean? Take care of what?" John liked the way she bent into him, kissing him, smelling good.

"Take care of her," she said in a soft low tone. "You've got a plan. I know you do. And I'm the one who is going to help you with it. We'll have to see where she's staying. That was Bourke's Mercedes she was in, so she can't be too far away."

"Hold on, Marla. I don't have a plan. I don't know what you're thinking, but it can't be good. Can it?"

"Yes. You'll see. Give it some time. You always come up with something, Jack. Look how you handled that overblown sheik. He'll be eating out of your hand on the next sale."

"Yeah, I was pretty clever, wasn't I?"

"You sure were, Jack. He won how many races with that horse you sold him a few months ago?" She took his hand, squeezed it.

"Three races I know of. Yeah, you're right. Lots. He won lots. He owes me now."

"He does. And you made a fat commission on it, too," she said. "It will keep us for at least a year, Jack. Don't screw this up."

"A year! Marla, are you nuts? It will keep us for five years after the money I skimmed off the top. The sheik will never figure it out. I am the best broker in Ireland." He laughed and said, "That was easy, and the next one will be easier. I know exactly how to play him. Heard there's action in Mexico, too."

"Mexico?" she said.

"Yeah, they need good brokers. I'm the best, so it's a done deal. We can make a lot of dough if I can get connected. We made a ton on that sheik and he's good for more, but I have to expand. Keep things moving."

"Yes, that's true. Good thing you stashed that money in a safe bank," she said climbing into the truck.

He got into the driver's seat of the truck. "Wiring the money into that Swiss bank account of yours was brilliant. They'll never find out. It's not even in my name."

"I did what you asked me to do, Jack. It was all your idea. You're the master mind." Marla pulled out her cigarettes and offered him another one. "It's our little secret."

Nodding, he took it, saying in a loud voice, "Yeah, I am the master mind, aren't I? Let's go back to my house—think up a new plan. Have a little fun." Jack pulled onto the street and headed for the coast. "Yeah, I'll come up with something. Maybe we can get rid of her. Scare her into leaving." He flicked the cigarette ash out the window, smiling as he drove.

"I knew you'd think of something, Jack," Marla squeezed his arm. She pulled down the visor, looked into the mirror, and put on red lipstick. "Drive fast, Jack, I can't wait. Remember, I have to be home early tonight. My mother is so sick. I wish I didn't have to go home to let the caregiver go. We only have a few hours."

"Yeah, I know you told me over and over. We'll figure something out. Laine is not gonna mess up our plans. I've got a lot of money at stake. She's in the way, but not for long." He jammed the accelerator to the floor of the truck. It bumped along the road out of town as the wind swirled the smoke inside.

"That's how I like you to think. Straight ahead." Marla watched the road from her rear view mirror. Dust flew from the tires. No one was following them to Jack's place.

TEN
A YEAR EARLIER
GROSSE POINTE, MICHIGAN

John said in a hard voice, "I need the time by myself, Laine. I'm sailing alone. We'll celebrate your birthday another time."

"I want a divorce." She hung up on him.

"Bitch," he said, but felt like saying worse. Now he poured Scotch from the crystal decanter, gazing at Lake St. Clair from his window. He guzzled the liquor and poured another one. It made him feel good.

The doorbell rang.

"Damn it," he muttered. "Who could that be?" He flung the door open.

An elderly white-haired man holding a small suitcase stood on the front porch of the red French provincial house under the gray wrought iron balcony.

"What do you want?" John said.

"Sorry to bother you, but is this Laine Sullivan's home?"

"It is." John heard an accent.

"Um," the man hesitated. "Well, I've come to see her."

"She's not here. Who are you?"

"I'm her Uncle Norbert Sullivan. From Ireland, I am."

"Oh yeah? Laine's never mentioned any relative in... where'd you say?"

"Ireland. She's never met me."

"Oh?" said John taking a sip of his drink.

"May I come in?"

"Why not?" He stepped aside and motioned the old man into the house.

Norbert set down his small bag and took off his cap. John watched him take in the marble foyer, suspended spiral staircase leading from the first floor to the second floor, the intricate French railings, and crystal chandelier.

"Come on in," John said in a slurred voice. "I was having a drink. Want one?"

"Sure, I might as well. I was up all night. Can never sleep on planes."

John took him to the library and went to the bar. "Neat or with ice?"

"Neat is grand." His gaze surveyed the built-in bookcases, Louis XV antique desk, and leather chairs. "'Tis a beautiful home you have here, lad."

"It's Laine's home, actually," John said. "I moved in after we got married."

"I didn't know she'd married."

"About a year ago—maybe more—who knows these days." John handed Norbert his drink and sat across from him in one of the club chairs. "What can I do for you?"

"When can I see her?" He sipped the drink and placed it on the table.

"Another week or so. She's in New York finishing some project. Designing the interior of a Trumpy yacht or something. I can't keep track."

"Feck it. I came to the States expectin' to see her. Didn't know she worked in New York—could've flown there instead of comin' here to Michigan."

"She has a studio apartment on Park and Fifth. Hardly ever see her myself."

"I suppose I could get the next flight out."

"I suppose you could."

Norbert set his drink on the table, eyes squinting at the edges. "I wish I'd known. I came to give her a present—surprise her. If I'd known she'd be in New York… I should have called before I left Donegal. I have a ticket home day after tomorrow."

"No problem. I can give it to her."

"It's most important that *I* give it to her."

"I can tell her it's from you." John emptied his glass, got up, and refilled it at the bar.

John eyed Norbert and watched him thinking. "Can you tell me what it is?" He swished the Scotch around inside his mouth. It made him feel good.

Norbert thought a moment, looked at him. "You look like a sound man."

"Laine trusted me enough to marry me." He laughed.

"Ah sure," he said, rubbing a finger over his upper lip. "I suppose I could mail it to her in New York, but I should give it to her in person. I want to make sure she gets it." He looked over at him again. "How about you give me her address in New York before I leave?"

"No need to do that. Whatever it is will be safe with me." John topped off Norbert's glass, splashing some of it on the table.

"I suppose you're right. It seems a long way to come for nothin'. I wish I'd known she wouldn't be here." He stretched out his long legs, sipping the drink.

"I'll tell her you were here. She'll be sorry she missed you."

"Possibly, but we've never met. Her father and I were brothers, you see." Norbert was silent a moment. "He and I had a misunderstandin'. That's why he left Ireland and I stayed." Reaching inside the breast pocket of his suit coat, he said, "'Twas a long time ago." He pulled out a fat white envelope. "Laine is the last of our family line. I want her to have this." He opened the document and smoothed it on his knee.

"What is it?" He was very interested in the old man now. A document could only mean one thing—money. And he needed more of it—a lot more. He flopped down on the chair near him.

"A deed for her property in Ireland." He handed it to John.

He grabbed it a little too quickly. He'd have to loosen up or the old man might get suspicious. "Property? Laine has never mentioned property."

"Aye. She doesn't know she has it. I'm giving it to her."

"Where is this property?" John was feeling happy now. Better than he had in days.

"Blacksod—on the west coast of Ireland. Not far from Donegal—if you know where that is."

"Vaguely. How much property?"

"Oh, quite a lot along the coastline. Enough to secure her future, so it is."

John skimmed through the pages devouring the contents. "This is a very generous gift. Nice of you to give it to her."

"Look at me, lad," Norbert said with a chuckle. "I'm an old man. I don't have many years left, no kin save Laine. And like I said, she is the end of the Sullivan line. The property rightfully belongs to her—not to the state, where it would revert, if I didn't give it to her."

"I couldn't agree more," John said, concealing a smile. "I'll put it in the safe, if you want to leave it here for her." He popped up from the chair and went behind the bar.

Norbert said, "That's grand."

He slid a large photo to the left, exposing the safe. "This is Laine's sailboat crossing the Mackinac Island race finish line," he said, pointing to the picture. "Took first place." He dialed the combination, opened it, and slipped the deed inside. "Done," he said, slamming the door, readjusting the photo.

Norbert rose and said, "Well, then I'll be on my way. Thanks for the jar."

John remained silent a moment. He could not let him leave, before he found out more. "What are your plans for the weekend, now that you've delivered the deed and Laine's not here?"

"None. I thought I'd be spending it with her. My ticket home is not till Monday night." He started toward the foyer. "Can you call me a cab?"

"If you want one." John finished his drink, making a decision, following close behind him. "Say, Norbert, I was about to go for a sail. Why don't you join me? Yeah, since Laine's not here, why not? You don't leave for a few days anyway. C'mon."

"Sounds temptin'."

"Laine's boat is at the yacht club down the street," he said blocking the door." All fitted out, stocked—ready to go. I was going by myself for a couple of days, but it would be much nicer with company." He thought about how he had just told Laine he wanted to go alone—what a joke on her. He had stepped into a gold mine—he'd take the old man sailing— what a sail it would be. To hell with her—he had land now. Land in Ireland she knew nothing about. "Well, what will it be?"

Norbert said, "I don't swim. Wouldn't be much help to you."

"We're not going swimming, we're going sailing. Besides I can take care of that. Plenty of life jackets aboard." Jack thought, I might be able to get more information from him.

"I don't have the clothes for sailin', lad. I didn't expect to stay but a few days."

"You'll be back in time to catch your plane. It's only for the weekend. What time is it you leave?"

Norbert fumbled in his inside coat pocket, adjusting his glasses. "Looks like I leave Monday night, half nine. Me friend Margaret's pickin' me up when I land." He put the ticket back in his pocket. "Usually I call her when I change my plans. No need for that if you're sure we'll be back in time."

"I'm sure. Wait here." John tossed his drink down then dashed up the stairs. A few minutes later he returned. "Here," he said, "Try these sailing clothes on."

"No, lad."

"Try 'em on," John said in a loud voice. "There's the bathroom." He showed him it.

"You're crazy. I've not been sailin' in I can't tell you how many years. Even then I was terrified of the water."

"I can handle the boat alone. You can sit back and enjoy the ride."

Norbert thought a moment, took the clothes. "I'll give it a go."

While Norbert changed from his travel clothes, John opened the safe, pulled out a roll of bills, and his American and Canadian passport. He smiled as he removed the deed, stuffing it, and the rest of the items, into his duffle bag. Setting his cell phone on the bar, he washed the glasses and cleaned up. He went to the garage and threw Norbert's suitcase and his duffle in the trunk of the car.

Now they were walking out, climbing into the car and heading to the club for a two night sail. The sun was shining and there was a good wind—a good day to go sailing.

ELEVEN
LAKE ST. CLAIR

The sail on Lake St. Clair and up through the South Channel was uneventful, as engine, sails, and galley functioned amazingly well. John plied the two of them with plenty of liquor, winds had been favorable, and John's cooking was at its culinary best in such close quarters. They passed the two evenings playing gin rummy—John let Norbert win most games—or sitting topside admiring the wonders of the stars. He liked the old man. And his land.

They anchored near Harsens Island in a small inlet never touching land and watched the freighters pass by, sucking the current in and out of the channel. The tall, brown grass lined the rocky shore, and seagulls flew overhead on the nearby Canadian shoreline.

Norbert commented many times, "John, me lad, 'twas a great idea of yours. I've not been so relaxed in many a year."

"We've had good luck," he said, and lit a cigarette. He leaned back against the rail, guiding the wheel with his other hand. "Want one?"

"No, thanks just the same. Never got in the habit."

"It's not so bad out here. Wind is picking up a little, but not much to worry about."

"That's good. I have to catch that flight tomorrow."

"You'll be home on time. Don't worry." He sucked the smoke into his lungs and felt himself relax. "My last one," he said and chucked it into the lake. "You're a good influence."

"Glad you be likin' it." He sat against the wall nearest the galley, legs sprawled in front of him and gripping the safety rail.

The rest of the day was smooth sailing and they made good progress, until John changed course.

TWELVE

On Sunday morning, they arrived opposite Squirrel Island in Canadian waters. A strong wind blew and they tacked several times to stay in the South Channel. John hadn't planned to go as near to the rocks as they were headed, but an idea came to him. He wondered if he could get close enough to the shore to…

"We'd better be headin' back, lad? This wind is makin' my stomach a bit queasy. Those rocks up ahead are stickin' out like arrowheads. You sure this is deep enough?"

"Yeah, we're fine. I can come about and we'll steer clear of them. How about we spend tonight ashore and head back in the morning? I have camping gear below, if that would make you feel better or go to that small motel beyond the grassy area."

"If you think we'll make the plane tomorrow, it's good with me."

"Will you stop worrying about your plane? I told you I'd get you back in time, and I will. There's a motel there," John said pointing to the tree lined rocky shore.

"I can't make it out. It took us two days to get here, lad."

John needed to distract him or he may have a problem. "We'll make it home in a day—the wind will be at our back. Or we'll motor back. What do you say?"

Norbert eyed the deserted shore. "If you say so, lad. You're the captain." His face was creased and burned from the sun, peeling. "I could use a little ground under me feet."

John aimed the boat for the rocky coast ahead. He shivered under his flannel shirt. "Take the wheel a sec, will you? There's a lot of debris out here today. Watch for submerged telephone poles or drift wood—sail around it."

"Take the wheel?"

"You'll be fine."

"I'd rather stay in a motel, if that's alright with you. I'll pay." He moved to the wheel, gripping it between the spokes.

"Now you're on. You can't really see the motel from where we are, but it is just around the bend. The sea grass blocks the entrance to the marina. Head for the large rock ahead, and we'll be on course."

"Head for a rock!"

"Steer dead ahead. It's getting cold, so I'm going below to get the foul weather gear. I'll just be a minute." He disappeared below into the galley.

John returned to the stern and watched Norbert gripping the wheel, frowning, eyes squinting at the corners, steering the boat toward the black pointed rock.

"I'll take the wheel," he said. He tossed the yellow foul weather jacket to Norbert. "Take off your life jacket, Norbert. Put that on, it's warmer."

Norbert struggled out of the life jacket, dropping it on the deck. John heeled the boat over riding the wave. Norbert slipped a little grabbing the rail and sat down.

"Take it easy," he said.

John spun the wheel heading the bow off the wind.

"Getting a bit rough."

"We can handle it," John said. He was wondering what it would be like to own property in Ireland. The thought grew as the wind filled the sail and heeled the boat over on the port side. He could own that property all by himself—his own land. Why did he have to tell Laine? She'd never know the difference—it could be his little secret. Yeah, he didn't need to tell her. He stared at the only thing stopping him.

"Do you feel up to lowering the jib, Norbert?" John said in a loud, excited voice. "It's easy and we can make better time. We'll motor from here."

"Och, sure. I can try." He zipped up the heavy slicker and hesitated. "Hand me my life jacket."

"Skip it. You can put it on when you are finished dropping the sail. I need that jib down. Hurry, will ya? The wind's picked up." He steered away from the wind making it easier for Norbert to climb up on top of the cabin. "We have to do it now before the wind shifts."

"Aye." He frowned but crawled onto the foredeck and made his way to the mast. "This one?" He pointed to the jib. John nodded and he unfastened the line. The jib dropped, and the sail billowed in piles around his feet, tripping him. Norbert bent to free himself, letting go of the mast.

Jack smiled and steered the boat into the wind. The waves hit them broadside, shoving Norbert half off the boat, legs dangling close to the water. He was tangled in the sail and the lines. He lost his footing as the boat lurched and the bow dipped under the waves. Water sloshed over the foredeck while another wave surged against the side of the hull. Norbert flipped overboard, smothered in the sail.

"Help me!" Norbert bobbed up through the mass of white, but the sail slipped through his grip. Waves forced it down under the water as it wound tightly around his back pulling him with it.

"Grab the sail." John shouted to him. "Hold on to it!"

"Help me!" The waves washed over his head and he spit water from his mouth. "Help me!" He gripped the sail as it slid under the waves. Up again and down again he went, gasping for breath.

John watched in fascination as wave after wave hit him, loosening his grip on the sail. It stretched out like a thin current streaming away from the boat, filling with water, pulling him under.

"Hold on." he said in a hard voice. He knew what to do. He set the boat into the wind to give him time. "I have to cut the sail. I'll get to you." He scrambled to the foredeck and to the line that held Norbert to the sail. He cut it with the knife he kept in his jacket pocket, freeing it from the boat.

"I can't hold on much longer. I can't swim." He choked out water and held on to the sail as he floated further and further away from the sailboat under John's watchful eyes.

"I'll be right there." he shouted. "I'm coming." He thought about the land—the property—his land. It would be really nice to have a new start. Alone. He spun the wheel in the opposite direction away from Norbert.

He watched Norbert scream to him as another wave rolled over his head. John shouted he was coming as he sailed away.

The last of the line and the sail slipped quickly away from the boat and took Norbert under the waves with it. He bobbed up after an attempt or two, but John was too far away to see what was happening to him. Poor old man, John thought. He's lived a good life.

John smiled and stared at the Canadian shoreline. He envisioned the property in Ireland—green, beautiful. He could broker horses there like he did in New York. He knew the business—yes that's what he'd do. Live there and broker horses. Have a fine life. Setting the automatic tiller dead ahead, he made his move without a backward glance.

THIRTEEN
SQUIRREL ISLAND, CANADA

A few hours later, after John had disappeared into the woods along the Canadian shoreline, Claire and Michael Gudffin strolled along the beach path near the tall grass on their lakefront Squirrel Island property. The June evening was punctuated by the trill of a marsh wren, while sand pipers poked their long beaks into the rocky shoreline searching for food. As the warm summer breeze turned the leaves of weeping willows over and over, the current on the rocky shore swept pebbles along their path onto the beach.

Squeezing Michael's hand as they walked, Claire said, "We have all summer to ourselves. Seems strange without the family."

"I know. We'll miss them. But they have their lives too, Claire."

"What'll we do without grandchildren to watch—and meals to cook?"

"I'll have time to make some fishing flies," Michael said. "I hear the fish are really biting in the flats. We can go fishing."

Claire picked up a few stones and held them on her palm for him to see. "Yes, there is that. Found some quartz."

"I see," he said, taking a few from her. "We'll put them in your garden." The sunlight shone on the pink surface of the quartz as he turned them over.

"I see a few more up ahead."

"Let's check the dinghy while we're here."

As they approached the wooden dock, she said, "There's a few logs washed up on the beach."

"Let's pull them in, so someone won't run into them with the boat."

"Good idea. We'll use the line."

They picked their way around upturned kayaks and driftwood, waves slapping the odd-shaped logs.

Michael reached them first. He knelt in knee-deep water to fasten the line on the log.

"Oh hell," he said, "This is no log—it's an old man tied to a log."

"Oh my," she ran to him. "Is he alive?"

"I feel a pulse." Michael touched the man's throat, holding his fingers against the carotid artery. "He's hurt badly. Help me untie him. Looks like he was hanging on to the log for dear life."

"The poor man."

Together they unfastened the line that held him to the log and eased him onto the sandy part of the beach.

Taking off his jacket, Michael placed it under the man's head. "I'll get someone to help carry him up to the house. He's too heavy for us."

"Oh yes, go quickly," Claire said, smoothing the older man's wet hair from his face. "He's got a nasty wound on his forehead. Look here."

"We need a doctor. Wait here," Michael said. "Jerry and I can make some kind of stretcher to take him up to the house."

"Bring a couple of blankets."

"Okay, I'll be right back."

The man moaned and opened his eyes. Mumbling incoherently, he tried to speak.

"Don't try to talk," she said. "You're going to be alright." She placed her sweater over him. "Rest. We're getting a doctor."

Over the next year, they helped him recover. Slowly with their care, he progressed, but had no memory of what had happened to him. He knew nothing of his identity, but they did discover he had an Irish accent. The authorities in Ireland, Canada, and the United States were contacted, but nothing turned up.

The amnesia had wiped out his past, and he was searching for a future with their help. All he could remember was the name Margaret.

FOURTEEN
FROM DONEGAL TO BLACKROCK ISLAND
A YEAR LATER IN THE EVENING

Miles left Donegal, and he landed the helicopter on the island within a short time.

"We're here," he said to Laine, shutting down the engine.

"Enjoyed the ride," she said. "The area is beautiful."

"It is that. Let's go in."

They ducked against the torrential downpour to the front door of the lighthouse cottage. Shaking off raindrops, Miles introduced her to Patricia and Eamon, his caretakers on the island.

"Come in and dry off by the fire," said Patricia. "Your supper will be ready soon. But first I'll show you to your room, Laine, then bring you a lovely cuppa tea."

"I'd like a martini instead," Laine said, following her down the hallway.

"That you'll have. I'll tell Miles," said Patricia.

The shutters slapped against the cottage as they entered her room. "Och, the shutters bangin' against the place are givin' me a headache. I told Eamon to fasten 'em down this mornin', but he forgot with all he has to do. He'll have to fix 'em before we go to bed tonight, or they'll be no sleepin' in this place."

"I could sleep through anything. It's been a long day."

"Aye, lass, but not through this noise," she said in a light tone. "I'll be in the kitchen, if you need somethin'. We'll be eatin' soon enough." Placing bath towels on the bed, she left the room.

"I appreciate it." Laine saw the mass of dark clouds from her bedroom window. "I'll be there after I wash up."

When Laine got to the living room, Miles was on his cell phone. A voice from the speakerphone said, "Miles, where in hell are you? I've been lookin' all over."

"I'm on the island, Dodd."

Laine sat on the couch. Miles was frowning and running his hand through his hair, agitated.

"Well, you gotta get to the farm," said the clipped Irish lilt on the phone.

"I can't get off the island in this storm. You know that, Dodd. What's the problem?"

"Somethin' terrible is happened." Dodd's voice rose even louder in the room. "You gotta get here quick, lad."

"Hey, take it easy. What do you mean, something terrible has happened? What is it?"

"Rex is dead."

Miles inhaled sharply. *"What?"*

"Rex is dead. Shot in the back field on the farm. Found him there, we did."

"You're joking."

"I don't joke about a thing like that."

"Tell me, man. What the hell are you talking about?"

Laine, on high alert, anticipated something happening. Something was off.

"Look. Don't argue. I need you here. Don't be takin' your time, lad. Find a way to get here to the farm as soon as you can."

She saw the inquisitive look on Mile's face when he hung up the call.

"We've got a bad problem at the farm."

"I couldn't help overhearing," Laine said.

"My horse was shot. He's dead."

"That's awful." Laine set the drink down.

"Miles, what is that you say?" Eamon said as he walked into the room.

"Rex is dead."

"Not our Rex. I don't believe it," said Eamon. "Who the hell would do that?"

"For the luv of…" Patricia heard the news and ran in right behind Eamon, blessing herself and wiping her hands on her apron.

"We don't know. Best horse I had on any track—worth millions. Sadly enough, I sold him to the sheik's broker yesterday. He was going to be picked up tomorrow. What a disaster," said Miles.

"Why would anyone want to shoot your horse?" Laine asked.

"Don't know. He was a marvelous horse and worth every penny," said Miles.

"Only a bloody fool would do somethin' like it," said Eamon. Patricia nodded, keeping quiet.

"It seems senseless," Laine said.

"Yes, it's mind boggling. I can't get off the island until the storm lets up to find out anything. Maybe I can take the boat over to the mainland tonight. What do you think Eamon?"

Eamon jumped in. "You'd be daft to do that, lad, in this storm. Whatever it is, it'll keep till mornin'. It would be pure suicide."

"I've got to find out who did this." Miles swiveled around and faced him. "It can't wait until morning."

"Aye, but if you go tonight, you'll be dead, too. We've got a ragin' storm out there. Waves are over thirty feet high. Wind is blowin' enough to bend the trees over and touch the ground. You'd never make it in the boat—it'd be your death. Not tonight—wait till it dies down—can't last forever."

"I know you understand."

"I do, lad. You know I do." Eamon scratched his head. "We'll find a way. When it's safe."

The cell rang again. "Yes?" Miles said in a loud voice. "What is it, Dodd?"

"Didn't tell you before," Dodd said coming through the speaker. "Sean was on watch last night. Hasn't shown up for work all day—may have seen somethin'. We're lookin' for him. Not like him to be comin' in late to work."

"He the new stable boy?"

"Been workin' with us six months now. Good lad."

"I'll deal with him later. Have you sent for Wilfrid and Tom?"

"Aye, police cousins of yours are on their way. Called Vet Bronson," said Dodd. "When will you be here?"

"Soon as I can get off the island. The storm is making it difficult," Miles said in a strong voice. "I'll call you when I am on my way." Miles disconnected. "It's a damn northeaster tonight—just my luck."

"I'm so sorry," said Laine.

Miles, leaning his arm on the fireplace mantle and looking at Eamon, said, "I know it was fixed—like the others. Someone shot Rex to get back at me."

"Aye," he said. "But who?"

"I have my suspicions. I'll call some people and find out what I can. Someone wants my horses dead. If there's one thing I can do is put out my feelers. Could be that that damn sheik went off the grid—trying to get back at me, but it doesn't add up. I already sold several horses to him without any complaints."

"That's how the rich get richer," said Eamon. "Wouldn't put it past that slimy broker to try to get another one for a rock bottom price."

"You are right about that. I turned down an offer on another horse he wanted to buy last week—maybe he shot my horse to prove a point."

"Be careful," Eamon said. "Don't say another word. You're hurtin'—not thinkin' straight. Might be somethin' else goin' on."

"Like what?"

"Nothin', just rumors. Play it out till we get the facts."

Laine was not too sure what was happening. She didn't seem too sure about Bourke or Eamon right about now, either.

"We don't have any proof on any of it," said Miles.

"Not yet," Eamon said. "But we will."

Laine liked Miles, but didn't trust him from all this talk. Things were not adding up. She'd find out more by listening, so she kept quiet.

"Patricia, let's have dinner. I'm sure you are hungry, Laine, after the long trip," he said in a polite voice, albeit a bit distracted.

"It can wait, if you need to take care of this," she said.

"No, it's up to the police. We'll have to wait."

"Do you have any enemies you can think of?" Laine said in a soft voice. She could hear Max in her mind saying, "Get the intel."

"Not any that would want to shoot a poor defenseless animal of mine."

"I see," she said.

"Worse than terrible. It's a monster who'd be shootin' a million dollar horse," said Eamon.

"Let's not talk about it anymore, Eamon, until we have the facts," said Miles.

"If there's anything I can do…" she said, seeing Eamon nodding his head.

"Work on the lighthouse tomorrow," Miles said. "At least we'll make some progress on that, while I figure this out."

"Sure." She'd call Max with an update later that night. Miles seemed like a decent man, but she knew she was not a good judge of character—look what happened with John. She wouldn't be fooled again—if she could help it.

FIFTEEN
BLACKROCK

Around midnight, after they had eaten, the four of them sat in the main room in front of a small fire. They talked about the work they would do on the lighthouse in the morning.

"Laine, no need for you staying up on my account," said Miles.

"Yes, I think I'll get some sleep. Thanks for the lovely dinner, Patricia."

"Aye, be seein' you at breakfast, I will," said Patricia getting up from her chair.

"Eamon, let's fix the shutters," said Miles. "We could use a good night's sleep. The banging is driving me nuts."

"I'll be gettin' the tools. Start with this one here." He pointed to the front of the cottage, leaving the room. "Take a few minutes with the two of us."

"When do you think you can leave the island?" said Laine.

"As soon as possible. If I go tonight, I'll arrange for Eamon to bring you to the farm first thing tomorrow morning. You can meet the men who will be working on the lighthouse. I can take you on a short tour around the farm, if you want to see it."

"Sounds good. I am tired. I look forward to seeing everyone tomorrow. Hope it turns out well for you, Miles."

"Goodnight, then." Miles put on his foul weather gear and went outside to help Eamon secure the shutters. Patricia went to her room off the kitchen.

Later, Laine left an updated message for Max on his phone and got ready for bed. Wind howled outside her window as she lay in the soft down bed. She wondered about seeing John, Miles, the operation, and now—a dead horse. If her instincts were right, John was alive—but how could that be true?

Agitated, she yanked the covers off herself and got out of bed. Slipping on sweats, she opened the window. She heard the hum of a helicopter engine and the thumping of the rotor blades. Miles had to be leaving the island. It was time to take a late night stroll.

SIXTEEN
CARRICK'S PUB
BLACKSOD

While Laine was exploring the lighthouse tower, Jack was coming in from fishing in the dark in Blacksod Harbor. It was midnight and the weather had turned colder. He pulled the throttle into neutral and the old wood curragh drifted into the slip. He was drenched from the rain, and had a brown trout in the cooler. The engine idled as he secured the lines around pilings. Hiding the key on a hook underneath the seat, he thought about Laine. He pulled out a pint of *Bushmills*. Taking a swig, the liquor burned slowly and easily down his throat. He felt good, except for seeing his wife. *Why the hell was she in Donegal?* He took another swig. He felt fine.

Pulling out his cell, he punched Marla's number. "Meet me at Carrick's Pub in half an hour after you get your mother tucked in. Buy you a beer." He listened, "Yeah, I know it's late, Marla, but we need to talk." Nodding his head up and down, up and down, the current rocked the boat from side to side in the well. "Honey, I'll see you in less than an hour. Wear black."

She squawked in his ear.

He interrupted her. "Yeah, black tennis shoes and a black slicker." She squawked again. "Don't let it bother you. It's gonna stop by the time you get here. I'll be waiting for you at Carrick's Pub. Yeah, it's a dump—so what—it's a good place to meet."

He hung up, satisfied with the conversation, rubbed the stubble on his chin and took one more swallow. This time, it was smooth going down. He took another, swishing the liquor around his mouth. Before putting the bottle away, he slugged down another. He felt better as his insides warmed. A smile crept across his face. Marla had told him he was good at what he did. He believed her, and she knew just how good he was.

Throwing off the hood to his slicker, the rain peppered his face. He licked the salt from his lips. Stashing what was left of the bottle under the seat, he threw the loose lines in the corners of the curragh. The oars were left haphazard on the floor alongside of the seats. The last of his gear was stowed in the bow space. The pitch black sky over the Irish Sea didn't matter to him—he knew the water, and he knew how to navigate in any condition.

Now climbing over the side of the small eighteen-foot boat to the dock, it bounced up and down in the well. Tugging and pulling on the lines, springing back and forth, gave it life in the dark water.

He could not see the school of fish steering clear of the boat, slipping deeper into the kelp, but he knew they were there. He knew the water was muddy at the bottom, silt rising to the top. Kelp grew high and stringy between the rocks along the shore at the front of his slip—hiding places for the fish. Jack hesitated knowing this. Thinking about fishing in the dark excited him. One more fish before Marla showed up —naw, he'd have a few drinks in the pub instead. The dock creaked under his topsiders as he trudged down the wood planks. Murky water reflected under a single harbor light.

Nearing the bar, waves splashed over brown, red, and gray pebbles on the beach beneath his feet. They crunched as he walked toward the well-lit open entrance of the pub. Fascinated by a flicker of movement at the water's edge, he stopped and pointed his cell phone flashlight downward. Small silver and white-stomached minnows fought against the lapping waves on shore. The fish floundered in the turbulence and gave up swimming, flipping over and over on the wet ground. Crabs popping up from pebbly holes scurried aimlessly for new holes to dive into. He crushed the few remaining with his shoe grinding them into broken shells.

Smiling, Jack lit a cigarette, staggered, and zigzagged in and out of the waves, daring them to soak his shoes. His feet made a sucking sound on the wet sand as he danced away from the waves.

He liked when the cool water tagged his feet—it felt good. He'd order another drink at the pub.

Misty rain, followed by a warm breeze blowing in from the sea, changed the weather in his favor. A moist film covered his skin. He felt refreshed—alive. When he entered the pub, he had a new thought.

"Hey, Jack, the usual?" asked the waitress as he slid into a cracked leather booth in the corner of the smoky pub.

"Yeah, Aideen, two orders of bangers and mash. Rashers and a Scotch. I'm starved."

"Thirsty, too. You'll have your drink first," she said in a loud voice.

A few regulars tipped shots of whiskey at the bar. "Hey, Lafferty, too good for us tonight? We've got an extra stool over here."

He shook his head and waved them off. "Not tonight. Meeting someone." He wanted that drink. They were not good men—not at all brave. Wasted themselves and never caught any good fish. He had no use for them, except the occasional extra hand with fixing the roof of his house.

"Nobody you want us to know," said the unshaven man, slurring his words. "Bet on it."

"It's nothing like that, Charlie," he said. "I'm busy tonight."

"Yeah, Jack's too good for us," said the other man, spilling his drink down the front of his dirty t-shirt. "Can't sit with us cause you're too busy doing nothing." He puffed out his chest, raised both fists, wanting a fight.

"Don't make anything of it," Jack said, looking at his watch. "Hunt deer on my farm today?"

They slapped each other on the back and laughed as if he told a joke. "Not today. Callaghan brothers were at your place. We got called in to fix the stables at Ashford Castle, we did. Another day—you owe us, Jack." They turned back to their stories ignoring him, ordering more drinks.

"Pick a day," he said, checking his watch again.

Aideen brought Scotch. Slapped it down in front of him and left. News blared from the flat screen television over the bar. Newscasters mouthed the coming weather. He ignored them and sipped his drink.

"It's almost eleven. Where the hell is she?" he said in a low voice. The Scotch warmed him.

SEVENTEEN

After what seemed like half an hour later, in she walked, long-legged, with blonde silky hair bouncing.

"How'd it go?" she asked, sliding across from him in the booth.

"Not good. Keep your voice down," he said and scanned the room. He smelled her perfume, expensive. "Been shopping?"

She kept her voice low. "Yes, but that's beside the point. So what's this all about? You said you have a plan?" She yawned.

"Hold on," he said as the waitress placed the food in front of him. "Got any ketchup, Aideen?" he asked.

"Americans have to have your ketchup," she said in a sharp voice from the kitchen door. "Ruin a meal, you will." She stomped over to the bar and grabbed the plastic container from Danny who was wiping up the top of the counter with a dirty rag. "Anything else?" she asked, hands on her hips, round face beaming under thinning gray hair. "Want something?" She looked at Marla, frowning.

"No," Marla said, turning her face away.

"Another Scotch for me, Aideen. That's about it," he said, squirting a generous amount on his bacon.

"That's disgusting." Leaving them to eat, she thumped away, back bent over.

"So tell me," she said, jabbing a fork into his mash.

"Has to be tonight," he said as he jammed his mouth full of potatoes. "Oh yeah, and another thing, before we get into that… Rodriguez, the Mexican boy I met in the bar the other night—the one I hired to spy on Laine and Bourke—remember him? I told you about him at the racetrack the other day—you know after we…" He grinned, food showing in his mouth.

"Quiet. They'll hear you," Marla said, looking around. "So, what about it?" She grabbed his Scotch and took a long swallow.

"Well anyway, the Mexican boy said they're going to start ripping apart the lighthouse tower wall on the island tomorrow. My wife's decorating it or something. Damn crew is meeting her early in the morning on the island. Said she's staying in the cottage with the old couple. Mexican boy is getting her daily schedule for me."

"What are you talking about?" Marla said, taking another bite of his mash.

He went on without hearing her. "And another thing, the Mexican boy's got some cousin in the horse business in Mexico. The country."

"No kidding. So what?"

"Said his cousin buys lots of racehorses. Says he's going to fix me up with him—says he's got 'mucho pesetas.' Good, eh?" Jack kept chewing. Food shot out of his mouth and landed back on his plate. "I can broker horses for him."

"Jack, you brought me here to tell me that?" she said in an angry tone, putting down the fork, watching Jack eat.

"No, Marla. We've got to snatch Laine tonight. That's why I told you to meet me pronto."

"How are we going to do that?"

"Use the tunnels you told me about on the island. We'll be out of luck if they block them up during the construction." He belched, kept chewing, and downed the mash with Scotch.

"Tonight! You're not serious. How?" Marla stared at him. She flipped her hair over her shoulder. Pulling red lipstick from her pocketbook, she smeared it on her full lips making the left side higher than the right.

Jack didn't seem to notice.

"Drug her tea with arsenic. She loves her tea. I can sneak in and put a massive dose in her tea tin. She carries that damn thing with her wherever she travels. Drove me crazy."

"Sounds iffy," she said. "It'll never work. We don't have that kind of time to wait for the poison to take effect."

"I can use chloroform to knock her out, if we want to take her. I found some in an old bottle on the farm. I've got it in the boat. She won't know what hit her," he grinned.

"You've been drinking, Jack," she said looking around the room. "This is your plan?"

"Yeah, baby. We leave straight from here. Kidnap her. Drug her—give her arsenic—skip that—yeah it takes too long. We'll use chloroform and gag her. We can drag her through the tunnels to the boat and dump her in the ocean—the sharks can do the rest. It's simple."

"It's not simple. What if they hear us when we take her?"

"Naw. She can try to scream her head off, but I'll gag her. Like I said she'll be drugged." He wiped a drip of ketchup off his chin with his hand, wiping it on his shirt.

"Jack, what if we drug her and leave her in one of the caves? There's one down by the end of the harbor cove near the steps—it's where Bourke docks his yacht."

He hesitated, thinking.

"You can gag her, tie her up, and go back later to take her out in the boat—tomorrow night. We'll have more time to plan things. It'll give us more time."

"I already planned it," he said. He felt good inside—warm. He ignored her, "We're going tonight while it's dark." He scraped the last of his meal from his plate with his fork.

"I like my plan better, Jack," she said and reached for his free hand. "You're so smart, but the weather tonight is bad."

"It fine, Marla. Remember, we can be together if we get rid of her. She's in the way. They'll never know what happened to her. That's what you want isn't it?"

Leaning toward him, she exposed a full inch of see-through lace on her camisole under her half unbuttoned shirt. "Sure, Jack, I need a minute to think about this. I'm surprised you planned it so fast. How about we leave her in the cave tonight? Come back tomorrow night and dispose of her?"

His eyes never left her chest. "No, we have to dump her. By the time they realize she's gone, we'll own her land. And everything else she has. It will be all ours. Laine and I are still technically married, you know. Or did you forget?" His boozy eyes met hers.

"Don't remind me," she said in a hard voice. "Okay, tonight we start a new beginning. Let's go over it again. Where did you tell me you are taking her tonight?"

"*We* are taking her, Marla. *Us—you and me.* After I drug her and gag her—*we* are taking her to the boat. You and me are gonna dump her in the ocean. Remember? I explained it to you already. You need to show me how to get into that tower from the tunnels."

"No, we are going to put her in the cave and go back tomorrow."

"Oh yeah, I forgot that I have a new plan."

"Yes, you do. The steps are near the rock ledge leading into the tunnel. It will take you to the lighthouse tower. It's simple, I can draw you a map. You'll be fine on your own."

"Nope, this a two person job. We—meaning us—carry her out through the tunnels to the cave. Done deal."

"What do you mean we? You keep saying 'we.'" She sipped his Scotch, leaving a red lipstick mark on the glass.

"I need you to help me. You can be the lookout, after I drug her. I can carry her."

"How will you do *that?*"

"I can place the chloroform over her nose and mouth. She will never know what hit her. Don't worry." He swiped the sleeve of his shirt across his mouth.

"I don't know, Jack. I have to get home—to my mother." She rested her elbows on the table, hesitated when she saw his look. "Yeah, okay. When do we leave? I have to call my mother. Tell her I'll be late. This better work, Jack."

"Call her. It's happening now. We're definitely leaving." He signaled for the waitress.

"Give me a minute," she left the table and entered the ladies room. After several minutes, she returned to the booth. "Can't wait," she nodded at him. "We'll be rich and the land will be all ours, Jack."

"You bet. All ours. We'll have the money from the horses, too. I got another deal going with Rodriguez, that Mexican boy. I'll tell you about that later. Lots of money—he knows a lot of heavy investors in the racetrack business in Mexico. One is his cousin." He downed his drink. Leaving the booth, he said in a low tone, "We're going to be living the high life, Marla. Might as well start now." He threw a hundred-dollar bill on the table.

"I'll be right there." Marla took her time following him. She remained at the table, adjusting her lipstick while Jack exited the pub. She stole a glance around the bar—she thought no one was watching her. Grabbing the tip, she stuffed it into her handbag and left a five-dollar bill in its place. Marla struggled into her black leather jacket and sauntered out of the pub.

Aideen saw Marla make the switch with her tip. She noted the time. Jack would hear about it the next time he was in. From the window, she saw them leave the harbor in his curragh—without lights—in a rough sea. She wondered where they were going.

EIGHTEEN
BLACKROCK ISLAND

Nearing midnight, Jack and Marla sped out of the harbor and bee-lined to Blackrock Island in the curragh. Light rain and dark clouds smothered the full moon as they neared the inlet beyond the point on the western shore of the island. Drawing closer, they could see the cottage lights and the lighthouse tower beam glowing above the black rock cliffs.

Marla said, "Jack I didn't bargain for this. How much longer? It's cold out here. I'm not dressed right."

"We're here, babe." Jack turned off the engine. The boat glided onto the pebbly shore, scraping the bottom on the rocks. Swinging his legs over the side, he slipped into the dark water, saying, "Grab the anchor. Hand it to me." She did with a grunt, and he wedged it into the beach.

"How am I going to get out, Jack? It's slippery." She wrapped her arms around herself.

"You'll be fine. Do what I did. Slide over the bow. I'll catch you."

"Ouch, that hurts," she said as her stomach caught on the bow cleat.

"Quiet. They'll hear you. Lift yourself off the cleat, Marla. I've got you." He grabbed both of her legs, pushed her up over the cleat, and lowered her into the knee-deep water.

"My good shoes, Jack. I'll ruin my shoes. I bought these shoes today. Oh my God, the water is freezing."

"I'll get you some new ones," he said in a strong voice. Grabbing her hand, he pulled her onto the shore. "Come on. You're okay."

"No, I hurt myself, Jack. Look—my blouse is ripped. My shoes are soaked—this is nuts."

"I'll get you a new shirt. We've got to get going. Stop complaining."

She rubbed her stomach. "Let's get this over with. I gotta get home—to my mom."

"Yeah, yeah, yeah," he said, picking a path along the rocky shoreline. Marla followed.

Trudging along the rocky, uneven beach, they made their way to the point. Around the next bend, Miles' boat was docked in the cove, and along the dock leading from it were the stone stairs to the tunnels.

In the shadow of the yacht, Jack said. "Wait here. I'll be right back."

"No way, Jack, I'm going with you. I see the steps. Over there," she pointed ahead to the right. "I think they'll lead us to the tunnels."

"What do you mean, 'you think'?" He stopped and put his face close to hers.

"You smell like Scotch, Jack. Get out of my face. Move it or I'm leaving." Pushing him out of the way, she said, "I haven't been here since I was a kid, so I have to make sure it's the right place. I'll lead."

"Fine," he said and dropped behind her, watching her hips sway as she walked. They trudged along the rocky path.

"This is definitely it," she said.

"Well, let's get going. We don't have all day."

They climbed the stone stairs to the top ledge within a matter of minutes.

Marla shined her light over the rocks. "The entrance is here somewhere. Got it." She hesitated, letting go of his hand, flipping her red hair out of her face. "I'm not dressed for this. I might trip on my shoes."

A narrow black hole stretched in front of them.

"Come on, Marla. We've got to do this tonight, so I can collect the money and the land when she dies. Remember?" He pushed her in the back to get her moving.

"Stop it," she said in an angry voice. Her feet slid on the wet uneven stones, and she fell. "Jack, what's wrong with you? Help me up."

"Jittery, I guess. Didn't mean to knock you down, Marla. Here, take my hand." He beamed his light in her face and then on the walls around her.

"Get the light out of my eyes. I can't see." Marla pulled herself up with the help of Jack's hand. "That's it. I've had enough." She turned to go back the way they came.

Jack caught her in an embrace and kissed her hard. "Didn't mean it, Marla. It was an accident. Show me how to get to the lighthouse. Come on. Will you do that for us, Marla? I'll buy you whatever you want tomorrow—when we get back to the mainland. Anything."

"Well, alright, but stop shoving me. And remember, Jack, you said 'anything.'" She saw Jack watching her, smiling.

"Good," he said. "Can we go now?" He gave her a short peck on the cheek.

"Follow me," she said, shoes squeaking and squishing as she walked.

The tunnel was dark, and water seeped from mossy crevices. It smelled dank and rotten. They wound their way through the curves and forks, lights dancing in a circle above and around them. Marla played with the light and found the old path to the lighthouse tunnel. Several X's, painted in white, marked the walls leading the way. At the forks, the color would change to red, yellow, or blue.

"I think it's the red path," she said, taking it with Jack close behind her.

"I hope you're right."

"Jack, shine your light next to mine—right ahead of us. To the left."

A flurry of bats flew straight at them.

"Oh my God," she shouted. "Changed my mind—I'm out of *here.*" She turned and ran smack into him, knocking both of them to the floor. A thick mass of bats soared over their heads. "I've had it," she said, taking her arms from around her head and shoving herself off him. "I'm leaving."

"Hold on. They're gone. We scared 'em that's all, Marla," he said, helping her up. "Really, they're not here anymore."

"Neither am I," she said, limping away from him.

"Slow down will ya? We've got to get rid of Laine tonight. We're already here—give it a few more minutes." He gripped her by the waist, pulling her back to him, turning them toward the darkness. "For us."

She said, "No, no, no. We need a new plan. Something else—this place gives me the creeps. It wasn't like this when we were kids."

"We've come this far—it can't be much farther. Yes, we'll come back—like you said—make another plan. But I have to know how to set it up. Just a little longer."

"Fine, but then we're out of here," she said, returning to the way she had originally headed, slipping on the uneven stones. "Promise me, Jack, only a quick look—then it's adios. Better not be any more bats." She said it in an angry tone, moving along the tunnel, watching for movements ahead.

"Take your time," Jack said. "It's hard to see. Don't worry, I'll protect you." The light from the flashlight bounced ahead of them.

"Yeah, right, that I'd like to see," said Marla, voice hard. "Like you did a minute ago."

"Well, I wasn't prepared. I'm prepared now. Prepared to get rid of Laine, too," he said in a low voice.

"I'm hearing a lot of talk—it stinks in here. What's that smell?" She peered ahead of her. He shined the flashlight on the ceiling. It was an endless dark space ahead, and unfamiliar. "Sick. It smells awful."

"Yeah, it smells like something died." He shut his mouth when he saw her expression. "Bad air. This place doesn't get a lot fresh air." He bit back his words. It was only making it worse. Marla's face turned into a frown like he had never seen. He thought, I'm in trouble, better make up something good. "Hey, Marla, we can go to the racetrack when we get back. Bet on a few horses. I've got an inside tip from the Mexican boy, Rodriguez. Wanna do that?"

"Maybe… I have to concentrate, it's tricky in here."

Jack relaxed. Let her think. He kept his mouth shut.

Finally after a few minutes, Marla stopped walking. She said in a small voice, "I think we're lost. This doesn't seem right—it's taking too long."

She was talking to herself—not him, he thought. He got a bad feeling about it. He needed a drink.

"I remember going down the middle fork—following the red paint. We used to have a song about it. 'Red, red …' something or other. Can't remember—oh, well. Or was it yellow—to the right, let's fight, fight, fight?"

"What the hell we gonna do, Marla?"

"Who knows?" She shrugged.

"Stinks," he said, covering his nose with his hand. "Ever seen rats?"

"No, shut up, Jack. Enough is enough. I hate this plan of yours. Come on."

Marla led them down several more paths turning left, winding up and down the wet slippery rocks. Finally, after several minutes, they passed a wooden door on their right. A horizontal bar was fastened over it between iron slats.

"Hey, this is it," she said in a low tone. "We're almost there—a few more minutes. I know this place after all."

"Quiet. What's that?" Jack said in a low voice, grabbing her arm. "Maybe we should go that way? I hear something." He pointed back the way they came.

"No, Jack. It's the door to the pantry inside the cottage kitchen. We're alongside the lighthouse tower," she said in excited voice. "I can hear them talking. Come on, we're not far from the map room. I recognize this. We will be at the entrance of the tower at the end of this tunnel. Are you coming?" She shined the light in his face, laughed at his look. "How do you like it?"

"Hey, I can't see, Marla. Knock it off," he said in a low voice. He blocked the light with his hand while sweat poured from his forehead. He felt bad—thought about another Scotch.

"Follow me." At the dead end, Marla pointed to a rectangular outline embedded in the tunnel floor. "Jack, this is the hatch to the map room. I told you about it, remember? It leads into the tower through the fireplace. We're standing over a stone fireplace—right here." She shined her flashlight on the image of the hatch. "Open it. It's on hinges. I know it's heavy, so be careful. It took Miles and me both to open it as kids."

"You did this with Miles?" He rubbed his chin.

"Yeah, it was a long time ago. Fun playing in these tunnels—hide and seek, you know—kid stuff."

"It's hard to see," said Jack, not liking what he heard, scowling, and looking around. "I don't see any hatch."

"You're stepping on it, Jack. What's the matter with you? We're here—I told you—above the fireplace in the lighthouse tower."

"How do you know?" Jack saw Marla's mouth drop open.

"Are you kidding? I know these tunnels like the back of my hand," she said in a defensive voice. "Look. It's right there. Get off it." She played her light back and forth over the outline of the large stone slab hatch in the floor. "Open it."

"Open what? What is it, Marla?" Jack scratched his head. "All looks the same to me."

"What's gotten into you? Too much Scotch. Right there at the end of my light—the hatch, dummy—the one I told you about in the pub." She shoved his head down to look at it. "It's our way in. But don't fall down inside it once you flip it open."

"Oh *that* hatch," he said, pushing her hand away. "Yeah, I remember now. What do I do?"

"Are you serious? Flip it open. It's on hinges, but take your time. It's heavy."

"Looks heavy."

"That's what I said, Jack, *heavy.*" She shivered. "Come on, I'm cold. Hurry up, will you?"

"Quiet, Marla, I'm only gonna be a minute." He tugged at the rusty wrought iron ring, but it didn't budge. "How'd you get this thing open, anyway?" He tugged harder, fingers cramping. The hatch opened a crack. "Hey, it moved." Sweat ran down the sides of his shirt, soaking it.

"This is ridiculous. I don't know why I had to come if you can't even get the thing open. You dragged me here for nothing, Jack."

"Hold on, will ya?" He groaned. It moved a few more inches. "The hinges are rusty." He squatted on the floor, straddled the slab between his legs, and pulled on the ring. Gripping the hatch on either side in the middle, he pulled as hard as he could. It gave and fell backward on his lap, pinning him under it. "Holy frickin' crap." He choked out a scream. "You've gotta be kidding me."

Shoving it slowly off his lap, he scooted backward. It slammed on the floor. Curled up in a ball, he held his hands between his legs, breathing heavily. "I wanna die, Marla. You should've told me it was *that heavy.*" He rolled onto his knees, squeezing his eyes shut. Rising slowly, he bent at the waist, sucking in air.

"Get over it, you weren't listening. Let's get this done. And *stop* complaining. Why it had to be tonight is still a mystery to me."

He said in a raspy, hard voice, "Tonight? Are you for real? I needed to know the layout if I'm gonna kill her. And we had to come this time of day, princess, so nobody would see our boat. It had to be tonight in the dark. You have no feelings."

"I know." Marla rubbed her arms, looking through the large opening into the fireplace below. "Are you okay?" she said in a soft voice. "You did it, Jack, I knew you could."

"Yeah, I did." Jack felt better. Sweat rolled off his nose. He shined his flashlight into the fireplace below. Next, he lay on his stomach, looking closer at the space.

"Dark in there," he said. "Hold on." Flipping off the light, his voice became a whisper. A light went on in the room below them. "Shhhhh— I hear somebody."

Marla knelt next to him, peering into the space. "See anyone?" she said in a soft voice.

"I hear someone talking. *It's Laine. My wife.*" In a whisper, he said, "Shut up."

They scooted away from the opening, pressing their backs against the wall of the tunnel. The gaping hole revealed light coming from below and Laine's voice.

"Oh, I…" Jack put his hand over Marla's mouth to silence her.

He whispered, "She's in the map room. We can nab her now."

"How?" Marla said in a whisper. "We don't have anything with us."

"Let me think," he said into her ear. "I've got it."

NINETEEN
BLACKROCK LIGHTHOUSE

While Marla and Jack hovered in the tower tunnel above the fireplace, Laine walked into the map room below them.

"I've got my work cut out for me," Laine said in a loud voice, setting her mug of tea on the refectory table. "This place is a mess."

Lights flickered on and off, casting dark shadows along the peeling stucco walls. She took in her surroundings. "Since I can't sleep, I might as well see where we'll start tomorrow." She checked the time on her cell phone—midnight.

"What's all this?" Stepping over piles of debris near the table, she made a mental note to clean the place. "Good God, this fireplace could swallow a whale." She peered into the black hole of the sooty stone fireplace. "Bet this hasn't been cleaned in years," she said out loud and laughed, knowing she was talking to herself. "Dead birds, guano. What other kind of litter is on this fireplace floor?" Sidestepping yellowed newspapers, kicking dried orange peels and apple cores out of the way, she leaned away from the opening.

"I've got a big job ahead of me." Slumping into a chair by the window, John came to mind—she knew it was him—there was no doubt.

"Better text Max," she said, pulling the cell phone from her sweatshirt pocket.

"Max?" said Jack in a loud voice. Marla elbowed him into silence.

Laine was startled by the voice. "Hello? Anyone there?"

Nothing.

She stood, and walked to the stairwell. "Eamon? Patricia?" she shouted down. Her voice echoed back to her. "That's strange. Thought I heard someone." She surveyed the room. "Must be hearing things."

Jack took a chance and hung the upper half of his body part way into the fireplace hole, peering below the stone opening, he could see her standing by the door to the stairs. He cupped his hands to his mouth and in a long drawn out whisper, he said, "Laaaaine." He dragged out the 'a'. He covered his mouth against a chuckle, and pulled himself back up inside the hole into the tunnel.

Marla punched him in the arm, and mouthed in a soft voice, "Stop it."

"Owe, that hurt," he said in a low tone in her ear, wrapping his arm around her.

"Big baby," she said in a whisper.

"Who's there?" asked Laine, her footsteps echoing on the floor. Laine said in a loud voice, leaning out the tower window, "Eamon, Patricia that you? I'm up here—in the tower."

No answer.

Jack and Marla hovered close to each other and waited in silence.

TWENTY
LIGHTHOUSE MAP ROOM

Laine leaned part way out of the tower window, looked down, and then pulled herself back into the room. Still no one answered. Spying the fireplace and the mess in front of it, she walked over to it again and tried to peer inside. A mass of cobwebs blocked her from seeing most of the inside of it.

"Disgusting. This has to be cleaned," she said in a high pitch. "It's going to be first on my to-do list. Bet they haven't had a fire in here in years."

Marla and Jack flattened themselves against the wet wall, pushing back away from the opening.

"Smells putrid," she said, clearing her throat. Soot and ash smudged her sweatshirt as she rubbed against the side of the fireplace. "That does it. Now I've ruined my clothes in this filthy place. Tomorrow won't come soon enough." A large spider dangled in front of her, landing on her arm.

"Yikes," she said in an anxious voice. She flung it off, and it scurried into a crack near her head. "I've had enough." Laine backed out from the opening as quickly as possible. On her way out of the room, she turned off the light and descended the spiral stairway.

Jack waited until it was quiet before removing his arm from Marla's shoulders. He said in a low tone, "Think she's gone. I'll check." He turned on the flashlight. "That was close," he said. He swung his legs through the opening, inching down the narrow stone notches on the inside of the fireplace wall. He peered around the corner. The room was empty.

"Yeah, thanks to you and your chanting," she mouthed down to him from the opening.

"I wanted to grab her. Finish what we came to do."

"Next time. Let's go."

"She's definitely gone," he said to Marla, who was watching him from the open hatch in the fireplace ceiling.

"Good, let's get out of here, Jack. Come on."

"Wait a minute." He stepped from inside the fireplace into the room. He brushed aside cobwebs, even wiping one from his mouth. He spied a mug on the refectory table, lifted it and sniffed. It was still warm and looked full. He said in a hard voice, "Typical. Hmmm, Laine's favorite tea, but she didn't drink it." He put the mug down. "Too bad I don't have any arsenic with me."

"You've seen enough," she said in a loud voice from the fireplace. "Let's go while we still can."

"Hold on." He ran across the room, taking the spiral stairs downward two at a time. At the bottom, he found himself in the room leading out of the tower. There was a second small door that led into the cottage. He cracked it open, hinges squeaking. Down the hall to the right, a light glowed from a doorway. He hesitated, and started to go toward it, but stopped when he heard Laine talking to someone.

I'm out of here, he thought and slid along the wall, back the way he came. He closed the door, hinges creaking louder than when he opened it. He took off running up the spiral staircase, taking two steps at a time until he reached the map room. In the next instant, he was scrambling up the notches in the fireplace and into the tunnel. He said in an anxious voice, "Let's get out of here. Hurry. She might have heard me."

Marla stood shivering. "What are you talking about?"

"Laine might have heard the door creak. Nothing to be scared about. I followed her into the cottage from the tower. She was down the hall talking to someone, but she didn't see me. Hold the light." He secured the stone hatch. "Let's go. Quick, Marla."

"Tell me you really didn't follow her." Marla took off in a run, flashlight leading the way, Jack following.

"Well it wasn't you that was following her, was it?" he said in a curt voice. "Let's get something straight. I'm here to kill her. Correct that...we're here to kill her."

Darting down the passageway, they wound through the long, dark tunnel, tripping on the uneven stones, until they came to the wooden door that went into the kitchen pantry.

"Stop," Marla whispered. "Listen. I hear voices."

"No, keep going." He saw her point the flashlight on a large wooden door in the tunnel wall. "What's that?"

"Quiet, they'll hear you. It's a secret door to the cottage kitchen pantry. We found it when we were kids."

Jack stopped and listened. "Good one. Yeah, I hear them, too."

They crept closer. Marla said, "What are they saying?"

"Will you shut up? I am trying to hear." Jack pressed his ear close to the crack in the wooden frame. "A woman is saying they're leaving in the morning. A man is talking now."

"Can you make out what he's saying?" Marla crept next to him.

The loud man's voice said, "I'll check in the mornin' 'round six to see if the lass will be up. Miles is gone."

They exchanged glances. Marla motioned to leave, pointing toward the tunnel exit. Jack held her arm, not moving, shaking his head. "Wait. Let's see what else they say."

They heard a woman say, "I'll be makin' the lunch in the mornin' for the crew that's comin'."

"Aye, I'll be pickin' them up on the mainland around eight. Laine wants to come, too, so she can see Miles' stables, and meet the men. Be leavin' early, I will, luv. Better check the boat and lockup now."

"I'll be goin' to bed. Morning will come soon enough."

"Be back in a tick," the man said.

"You do that."

Marla and John watched the light go out in the crack around the door.

"We gotta get outta here, quick," Jack said to Marla, and shoved her forward.

"Don't push me, Jack. What's the rush?"

"Didn't you hear him? He's going down to check his boat. He might see our boat—just our luck. Nothing but trouble is coming. Which way do we go, Marla? Make it fast."

"Don't get your jeans in a twist, Jack. I know this tunnel like the back of my hand."

Jack gave her another shove. "Yeah, I bet you do. Hey, I've got something to tell you. Ever hear of that guy from town? Norbert something or other? Now there's a story."

"Tell me later."

He ignored her. "This is good, you'll like it. About a year ago, I was solo sailing on Lake St. Clair in Michigan in the States."

"Jack, I have to concentrate."

He continued in a low voice. "I invited this old guy, Laine's Uncle

86

Norbert, to go sailing with me. That is—after I found out he was giving her the deed to his property here in Ireland."

This got Marla's attention, she stopped, and turned around toward him. "Go on." He spun her around and pointed a sharp finger in her back to move her forward. "Walk and listen, will ya?"

"That hurt," she said in an angry voice. "Stop it. I'm listening. That's all I do is listen."

"Yeah right. Well, Norbert and I went sailing in Canadian waters. I had plenty of liquor, winds were favorable, and we ate aboard. No one knew we were out there, or that he came to see Laine—except me—and now you."

"So what? What happened?" Marla's flashlight played on the floor, making figure eights racing along the tunnel.

"We spent two evenings playing gin rummy—I let him win most games, got him to…"

"Is that really important?" she interrupted him.

"Sure is—you know, got him to trust me. See, the best part was he didn't swim and I had him on a sailboat."

"No, I don't see, but I know you'll tell me," she said sloshing along.

TWENTY-ONE
JACK'S STORY

"We anchored near Harsen's Island," Jack said continuing to tell his story about Norbert to Marla. "It's deserted there most of the time. We never touched land. Lots of marshes filled with grass along that shoreline—Indian country. Freighters come and go, but they don't take any notice of sailboats, unless you're in their way—which we weren't. You getting the idea?"

"If this story gets any longer, I'll fall asleep while I'm walking."

He continued in a light voice, liking the way she played the light. "Anyway, Norbert commented many times saying, 'John, me lad, 'twas a good idea of yours to get out on the lake sailing. I've not been so relaxed in many a year.'"

"I got him real relaxed. Called me, John. That's my real name, John Rafferty."

"What? No kidding." Marla's patience was running out. "Tell me the rest later, Jack, John or whatever your name really is," she said in a hard voice. "And it's obvious, you've had too much to drink tonight. I can clearly see that."

"Yeah, but Marla, I need to tell you the rest. Come on. Play along."

"Oh alright. I have nothing else to do right now except freeze my bum off in this smelly, dank tunnel."

"Pay attention. On Sunday morning, we got near Squirrel Island in the Canadian waters. It was rough. Windy, too. Norbert said he wanted to head back to Grosse Pointe. Something about his sea legs giving out. That was a good one," he laughed.

"Sea legs?" Marla flipped her hair and kept going. "Right."

"Can you imagine? Marla, I didn't have a plan at that time, but it came to me."

Jack's eyes narrowed, remembering. "I told him we'd spend the night ashore. Told him there was a marina and a motel near it close by on land. He said I had a good idea going there—even called me 'Captain' John. I liked that—I even liked him."

Marla said, "I hear the ocean, Jack, we're almost there."

Jack said, "I'm almost done with the story." Sweat rolled down his sides, soaking his shirt. "I made him take the wheel of the boat and head for a rock on the shore."

"Are you nuts?" she whirled around and he banged into her. "A rock?"

"No, it was a good direction. He did it, too," he stared into her eyes, smiling. "Next, I told him to lower the jib. We'd motor in. He crawled up there on the foredeck—no life jacket—dumb jerk. That's when I made it happen. It came to me in a flash. You'd have been proud of me, Marla."

"I'm sure I would have."

They took the stairs down to the inlet and made time reaching the curragh. Jack revved the engine and pushed off from the shore.

"This is the best part, Marla," he said as the boat moved out into the water. "I jibed the boat. Let the waves hit us broadside. Our port side was dipping the stanchions under the waves, wetting the deck, making it slippery enough, alright. I spun the wheel to make the boom reverse and slam into Norbert, knocking him overboard. Brilliant on my part, don't you think?"

Marla turned to him and frowned, nodding her head.

Jack went on not noticing while he steered away from the land. "He floundered at the surface of the water, bobbing up and down, gripping the sail I cut loose. He hollered, 'John, I can't swim. For God's sake, I can't swim, I can't swim.' It was a riot."

Marla wrapped her arms around herself and said, "I guess you showed him. Old fool."

"Yeah I did—he was an old fool now that I think about it. Waves and the sail dragged him under—then poof he vanished." His voice was loud. "In no time flat, I cleaned up the evidence, smashed the boat on the biggest rocks I could find. It was easy after that, I could walk to shore and I took off into the woods. No one saw me, Marla. It was perfect."

Marla listened to him talk, fixated on the waves spraying off the sides of the curragh.

She gripped the seat with both hands. "You bet it was."

"You would have been proud of me, Marla. You should have seen the look on his face when I turned the boat and sailed away from him—he couldn't believe it."

He smiled at her when she looked into his face. He knew she liked it by the way she stared at him, saying nothing. He continued in a strong voice, "The water near the shore was shallow, but it was hard to walk because it was rough. I could see ripples in the sand and fish feeding off the bottom. It was beautiful—colorful rocks—black, orange, gray. I jumped them, like stepping stones in a Bond movie. Got to the marshy shore, and sunk up to my knees in the muck. It smelled like dead fish. Thought I was a goner, but I managed to crawl out of it and head into the woods." Jack jammed the throttle forward as the boat slashed through the water, pounding the bow up and down in the waves.

"Slow it down, Jack," Marla said in a loud voice, spray drenching her, hair hanging limp, mascara running down her face.

"Can't. Got to keep ahead of them," he said. "Hang on." He sped on, shouting over the hum of the engine. "Hotwired an old Ford truck from some shack—might have been an Indian's junker. Lots of 'em on that island—Indians that is. And here we are, Marla—you and me. No more John Rafferty."

"There's no one by that name now." Marla hunched over while he wheeled the boat through the choppy waves.

"It was great. Wish you could have been there with me—just to see *that look* on his face. You would have loved it."

Jack smiled down on her in the dark night. Marla looked away as the boat headed toward Blacksod Harbor.

TWENTY-TWO
BOURKE FARM – LUCRE
BLACKSOD

Midmorning the same day on the mainland, silver and gray clouds covered the sun and swept over Miles Bourke's farm. Oats and wheat bent their tops in the wind, snapping them against the ground. Symmetrical stone walls housed hundreds of thoroughbred horses grazing in lush green fields. Narrow-winged Merlins circled overhead, their sharp, curved beaks eyeing the ground below.

Miles stood at the edge of the green pastures behind the stables and glared at the body of the dead horse. Young men dressed in shabby hunting gear, hands tied behind their backs, stood off to the side. Miles' hired hands cradled rifles in the crook of their arms and stood on either side of the disheveled hunters.

Wilfrid and Tom, the police officers and cousins of Miles, continued questioning the Callaghan brothers from Limerick while Miles listened.

"So where exactly were the two of you shooting?" said Tom.

"I told you," said the short shoddy hunter. "We was given permission to hunt there—right over there." He pointed to Miles' land.

"Place is not yours to hunt," said Wilfrid.

The Limerick men with round shoulders stood looking at their feet.

Miles said, "You had no right to be on my land. Why the hell did you shoot my horse?"

"We didn't mean to do it," said the youngest hunter with a full day's beard. "It was an accident. We didn't know it was a horse. We was huntin' deer—only deer. Had permission to be on the land."

"Accident, my arse," said Miles in an angry tone. "You had no right to be on my land or the land next door. It's trespassing."

The unshaven hunters nodded, faces sullen. They hung their heads, looking away from the dead horse. The policeman handcuffed the men's hands behind their backs.

"What will you do with them?" Miles face reddened.

"Take 'em in—judge will want to fine 'em. We wanted you to question them yourself—face-to-face," said Tom to Miles.

"What the hell's wrong with you? Can't you tell the difference between a horse and a deer?" shouted Miles, raising his fists, ready to spring on them. "Answer me."

The hunters looked at the ground. They said nothing.

"There's hell to pay—that horse was worth millions," said Miles. "You'll be paying it off for the rest of your life. Damn it, I have to call that crazy sheik and let him know his horse has been murdered. This is going to cause all sorts of trouble—thanks to you two." Miles ran his hand through his hair. "Gotta call that slimy broker, too, and get a replacement. Swore I'd never work with him again. Now—I have no choice. This is a disaster.

Oh hell… Get these jerks out of my sight."

"Miles, we'll take care of this scum," the police said. "Let's go."

"Let *us* be takin' care of 'em," said Dodd in a loud voice. "Make mince meat out of 'em."

"No Dodd, we'll be stayin' within the law. We're takin' it from here," said Tom. Donna worry, Miles, it'll never happen again. Be sure of that."

They shoved the men toward the police car. The hunters shuffled past the horse. Silent. Not looking. Pushing their heads down, the police directed the men into the back seat of the car and drove off.

TWENTY-THREE

Now Miles spotted Laine and Eamon coming up the dirt road toward him. "Hold up," he said. "I don't want you to see this. For God sake, Connor, cover him with something."

"Sorry, Boss." Connor retrieved several burlap bags and covered the horse's body.

Dodd said to Miles, "I've called the vet. Won't be long." He parked himself near the truck, eyes never leaving the horse.

"Stay with Rex until the vet comes. I'll check with you later."

Walking over, Miles said, "Eamon, you gather the crew. Laine and I will meet you on the island, after I show her the farm. Say in an hour?"

Eamon agreed and left them.

"Sorry you had to see this," said Miles.

"Yes," she said. "It's been a bad day for you today?"

"One of the worst." His phone rang and he answered it.

A few feet away, Laine heard Connor tell Eamon in a loud voice, "Callaghan brothers from Limerick shot Rex dead. Admitted it. Said they were huntin' on the neighbor's land next door with permission from a bloke named Jack. Wandered over here to Miles' property."

"Trespassin' it was," said Eamon.

"Thought Rex was a deer, they did." Laine watched him rubbed his hands together, speaking fast, kicking the dirt as he told it. "They dint know it was a horse. Make a man wonder what the hell's they shootin' at."

"Havin' a pint or two while killin' deer?" asked Eamon in a loud tone. "Bunch of loose screws, if ye be askin' me."

Connor shrugged. "Donno. What were they doin' on that property of Miles' anyway? 'Tis private land. The gents dint say nothin' 'bout whose land was wot," said Connor. "Says they was just huntin' and had a right to be here."

Miles hung up the phone. Overhearing them he said, "What was the man's name? Did you tell the police about this, before I got here?"

Connor came over to him. "Aye, we did. Callin' him Jack. Said they met him in a Blacksod pub. American talking man said he lives in the old Sullivan house."

"Sullivan house?" asked Miles.

Dodd pointed to the fields past Laine. It bordered Miles' land.

"Sullivan property all right. No one lives there," said Miles. "Hasn't for at least a year. They had no right to be on that land. Or mine."

Laine's head came up. She heard it—Sullivan property.

Connor said, "Aye, traded work for the yank, they did. Fixed the thatch on the roof of the main house, mowed the grass. Been overgrown. Complained a lot about that."

"I'll see about this." Miles' face reflected his rage.

"If you're finished with us, Miles, I best be gettin' to Rex," said Connor.

"Hold up a minute. Did you give the police the addresses in Limerick?'

"Aye, Tom and Wilfred put it in the report. Will be sendin' it to you."

Laine listened as tempers flared. Sullivan land—now this was a new one.

"Mark my words—those boys are going to pay," said Miles. "Killing my horse. Trespassing on my land…" said Miles. "Let me know when you've buried him on the farm. Same place all the other horses are buried, under the pine trees. Call me when the job is done."

Laine put her hand on his arm. "I can go back to the island with the crew, Miles. You have things to do."

"It'll get done."

"It's never easy."

"No, but since you are here, we can check out your property before you meet the crew. That is… if you want to. It was going to be my little surprise to take you over and see it."

"My property? I don't own any property here."

"Your family owns more property than anyone else on the west coast of Ireland."

TWENTY-FOUR
SULLIVAN PROPERTY

Leaving the men at the farm, Miles and Laine hopped into his rag-top jeep and headed north along a small path called the Fairy's Walk that took them to the Sullivan property. The rutted dirt road was canopied by thick foliage made of ivy. Fearnogs (Alders) and Fuinseog (Ash trees) formed a green tunnel surrounding the property. The wind was cool and the shadows deep.

Miles said, "The Druid's Circle is in the grove ahead." He motioned to it as they neared the circle of stones. "It's got a lot of history. I thought you'd like it."

"Yes, I'd like to see it." Laine remembered Stonehenge in England, and it reminded her of it. "It's a strange place." She reminded herself to call Max later. She would have to draw Miles out to find out more information.

"It is," he said and they climbed out of the jeep. "We used to play here as kids. Scare each other with stories. The fifteen stones surrounding the central boulder made an altar at one time. An altar for witches—bad witches. Irish legend, that it is," he said, and laughed.

"I like it. Do you know the history?" She surveyed the tall gray stones jutting upward toward the sky. Brown leaves covered the ground under bare trees.

"Not really. Animal skulls are perched on the limbs of the trees looking out on the road," Miles said. "Never liked this place."

"It's a splendid place, Miles, and so near to your horse farm."

"If you like dead things, I suppose it is. Not my taste."

"Speaking of that, I am sorry about your horse. How will Rex's death affect your business? I know it is none of my business, but this place made me think of it."

"Something is going on with this horse business. I don't want to burden you with it, but suffice to say, someone wants to ruin me—and my business."

"Horse racing and breeding is a cut throat business."

"Yes, and I am going to find out who is out to get me." His face turned hard and his voice was clipped.

"Look," she said, moving him off the topic. "There's a well over there." She pointed, seeing she was losing him with the conversation. "See steps leading up to it—under the trees?" She was looking across the road from where they were standing, away from the Druid's Circle. "Strange, the trees are green and lush over there—but not here. I see brambles, too."

Miles said, "That's the Wishing Steps and the Wishing Well. It's part of the legend that surrounds this place. It may be of interest to you. I have a book back at the lighthouse. You can read it you want to."

"Sure," said Laine.

"Time to go," said Miles.

The air from the sea filtered through the trees as they drove on. The fragmented rays of the sun were white against the shadows. Laine pictured the Atlantic Ocean, the cool green-blue of the water, whitecaps breaking on the surface. She felt good, despite the situation on the farm.

She said, "It is peaceful here."

"Yes. You are in the Belmullet Peninsula. The sea breeze is refreshing."

It was hard to focus on her mission—her objective, but she had to. She reminded herself to remember what happened—what's going on now. Keep asking him for information, she told herself.

"This is all Sullivan land. The whole coastline's yours." he said, driving over the uneven lane.

"I can't believe it. You have to be mistaken."

"Believe it," he answered. "It's been Sullivan property for generations. I've done the research. It's yours alright."

"That's pretty far fetched, since I don't have any relatives here," she laughed.

The spruce and oak trees pressed in on them, smelling of summer. As they passed an overgrown cemetery, Laine said, "Can we stop there? I'd like to look at the headstones in the cemetery. See if you're putting me on." She gave him a smile—knowing he was putting her on.

"Certainly, but don't say I didn't tell you." He pulled to the side of the road.

The cemetery was overgrown with tall grass and weeds.

Miles said in a light tone. "This is the Sullivan cemetery—a private cemetery on the Sullivan property."

"I don't believe you," she said, sliding from the jeep into the grass and wildflowers.

"Believe it," he said. "You sure are a tough one to convince." Miles turned off the engine and followed her through an unhinged rusty gate lying in the weeds.

"Oh, you're right. It says Sullivan. Unbelievable." She stared at the huge

Celtic cross mounted on a marble pedestal in the center of the cemetery. "I *could* be related to some of these people, but I highly doubt it."

"You are." Miles laughed. "All of them."

Laine looked at Miles watching her roam the area. "Not a chance."

She examined tombstones tilted over and others straight. Lilies and irises bloomed in scattered patches. Birds pecked at the ground and took flight as Miles and Laine approached them.

"They all say 'Sullivan.'" Laine said in a soft voice, "I don't understand."

"This is your land, Laine. I've been trying to tell you—your family has been here for years." He saw her frown. "I thought you knew."

"How would I know? No one ever told me."

"I'm telling you. Our grandparents were friends. They lived here—your grandparents, that is—in the main house where we are going. I assumed when I wrote my letter inviting you here to work for me, you knew the connection and about the land. About your family."

"Well, I didn't." She frowned, thinking back to Max's comment about her ancestors—he knew it all along. Why didn't he tell her? She was angry and he was going to hear about it. "This comes as a shock, Miles. It'll take me a while to digest this."

"I'm sure it will," he said watching her.

"Give me a few more minutes," she said in a low voice, thinking of killing Max. He had set her up with Miles. Knew about this property and used it for bait. She would have a lot to say to him tonight, but nothing to give him on this money laundering issue."

She wandered through the overgrown grass to a headstone with fresh flowers on it. Stopping in front of it, she read, "Norbert Sullivan 1935 to —. Who is Norbert Sullivan? Seems he is still alive. Someone put fresh flowers here."

"Norbert's your uncle. But—he disappeared about a year ago when he went to America. No one has heard from him since. Margaret must have put the forget-me-nots there. He lived in the house we are going to see."

"Margaret?" Laine asked with a lifted eyebrow.

"Margaret Hogan. She owns the title company in Donegal. They've been friends, or should I say companions, for years," Miles said. "You'll be seeing her soon, I expect. Have you seen enough?"

"Yes, but I would like to see the house you mentioned, if you have time." Laine was wondering where this was going. She would ask Max tonight.

"That's where we are headed. Let's go." He opened the door to the jeep.

"This is very strange. My parents immigrated to the States before I was born. They're both buried in Detroit. They never said a word about owning any property here or any relatives in Ireland."

"That is odd. Maybe we can shed some light on this mystery when we visit Margaret in town."

"I'd like that." It stopped her for a moment. She might have family she did not know about. Max would know—damn him. She had a lot of questions for him and he better have answers.

They left the cemetery, bumping along the road. The sun shined through gaps in the trees, and the sky was cloudless.

"Is it far?" she said in a light voice.

"Around the next bend. Patricia will have to tell you about the Banshee and the Fairy's Walk—the legends that surround this place."

"What's that?"

"Not what, but who—a feminine spirit— a banshee is a woman of the fairy mounds," he said, laughing at the look on her face. "And well… the Fairy's Walk… I'll let her tell you about it."

"Right," she said.

The place was becoming more interesting by the moment. Now the jeep wound down a small hill on the narrow road, bumping over the ruts. Laine gazed into the deep woods, listening to frogs croak from the stream that ran along the road.

Miles pulled up to a white stucco home with a red door, green shutters, and a thatched-roof. A profusion of primroses, sea holly, and harebell bordered each side of a winding pathway to the door. Wild flowers peeked above the long grass in a nearby field.

"It's exquisite," Laine said, "but isolated."

"And in good shape," said Miles. "Norbert kept it up. Not sure who is doing it now."

Laine surveyed the house, the sky, and the land. Skylarks warbled in the trees. The breeze blew cold, salty, sea air from the crashing waves on the shore.

"This is Norbert's house, but he actually lived in town." He paused a moment. "Jack could be the man who rents this place, if the hunter's are right. I don't think it's possible. Norbert didn't like strangers on his property. I am not sure I believe them."

"I see," she said.

Miles tried the door. "It's open. Let's have a look."

They entered into a large family room with a high beam ceiling. The smell of burned peat emanated from the open-hearth fireplace. A dark wood table surrounded by ladder-back chairs was off to one side. Antique plates filled the hutch near the table. Tapestry covered furniture was arranged in front of the fireplace.

"Nice place," Miles said. "It is definitely being used."

"Sure is," she said. "You've never been here?"

"Not since I was a child."

Miles walked into the bright kitchen and opened the refrigerator. "It's full of food." He opened a container of milk and smelled it. "Fresh—that's strange."

Walking to the sink, she said, "A lot of dirty dishes."

Miles opened a cupboard. "Someone likes his liquor. There's enough Bushmill's Scotch here for a Coronation. Expensive year." Miles shut the cupboard door.

"Scotch?" she said. Bad memories of John returned to her. She shoved them aside.

"I'd like to see the second floor." She returned to the parlor, and at the far end of the room, climbed stairs to the loft. "There's an office up here," she called down. "Lots of information on local horse dealers, horses sales, saddlery and tackle—enough *EQ Life* magazines to paper a wall. Ashtrays are full of cigarette butts—packages of Camel cigarettes on the floor. It stinks."

"Mess down here, too. First floor bedroom appears to be a man's room," Miles called up to her. "Bed's unmade, men's dirty clothes all over the floor. Someone is definitely living here."

Laine came down the stairs and went to Miles in the bedroom. From the door she said, "Needs someone to pick up after him."

On top of a dresser was a blue lanyard with keys at the end. She picked it up, examined it, puzzled. *Couldn't be,* she thought. "Miles, take a look at this. I had one like this on my sailboat in Michigan. The name's worn out. Do you recognize it?"

"None that I've ever seen. We use roped key buoys here in Ireland—in case you drop them in the water." He fingered the lanyard and set it back on the dresser. "Another coincidence?"

"Yes. I must be cracking up," she laughed. She had a funny feeling in her stomach.

"Doubt that. You might want to see the bathroom off the front room. I'm not sure what else there is to explore."

"It's actually clean. I'm shocked." There was an ashtray with cigarette butts, toothbrush and paste, and a black comb on the counter. She opened a drawer and slammed it shut. *Stop it.* Corduroy Cologne by Zirh International—the same cologne John wore. This is all too much like him. She began to doubt herself, until she saw him in her mind—in the square, smiling, with the other woman. Tonight, she would ask Max to find out about this house and about the man who was living in it.

"Ready?"

"Let's go," she said. "I've seen more than enough." She rubbed her arm by habit.

"Before I forget, the crew went with Eamon by boat to the island. They're waiting to meet you when we return. We can start construction on the tower today, if you're up for it. Patricia is giving them something to eat."

"Sounds good."

As they were about to leave the house, they heard a door slam and an engine sputtered and caught.

Miles ran to the front door and said in a loud voice, "Hey, you there. Hold up."

A dark blue truck raced down the gravel road, and vanished around the curve.

"Who was that?"

"I don't know, but we weren't alone."

TWENTY-FIVE
MCGINTY'S PUB
BLACKSOD

Dust flew from the tires as Jack left the Sullivan house in his dark blue truck. Now he was taking the back roads at break neck speed, avoiding Laine and Miles. In a short time, he got to Blacksod Harbor, jumped into his curragh, and sped out of the harbor. He needed the ocean to clear his head. The sun was past noon, and it beat down on his back.

Fishing for part of the time caught him nothing and drained his supply of Scotch that he kept aboard the boat. Guiding himself back into the harbor after an hour of trolling brought him no relief. He felt bad. No bites. It was a bad day.

Tangling his line in the engine made him cut the line. Tripping over his pole, he lost his footing and landed on the gas tank in the stern of the boat. The rod sprung out of his grip and flew into the water. He watched it sink to the bottom of the ocean, before he could snatch it out.

"Damn it," he said. "That was my best pole." He downed what was left of the half bottle of Scotch and threw the empty liter into the waves. He sneered as the glass mocked him by not sinking right way, dancing and bobbing up and down on the crest of the waves.

Docking was hard for him when he entered his well. The current was strong as the old wood boat bumped and crashed against the pilings along the dock when he pulled into the slip. Grabbing a fender, he tossed it over the starboard side. After looping a line around the tilted wood piling, he secured the boat before it surged forward onto the rocks.

"I've had it," he said in a loud voice. He tucked the key away under the seat and flipped the bumpers over the side. He climbed out of the boat and strode down the dock to the old fisherman in the next well.

"Been fishin', have you, Jack?" Kieran Breen said from his boat in the next slip over. The stooped man bent over the fishing nets, mending them by hand. "Working on me snap-nets, I am. On your way to be havin' a pull at McGinty's pub? Or Carrick's?"

"The fish aren't biting—got skunked. Bad day. A pint sounds good at McGinty's. Come along? I've had it with fishing today."

The dock creaked under his deck shoes and he took a seat on the dock near the fisherman's skiff, legs hanging a few feet above the water next to the other man's boat.

"Grand," he said, pulling the net over his knees in the cramped space between the planked seats. "Be wantin' a Jameson or two. Took the yanks out fly-fishing on Lough Corrib today. Said I was the best guile they ever had—what do they know? Caught us fourteen or fifteen kelts but no fresh salmon. Damn yanks jabbering the whole time. No offense."

"None taken. Any brown trout?' Jack said, lighting a cigarette, blowing smoke rings, sitting and swinging his legs from the dock.

"Aye, one Breac Donn, the biggest brown trout I'll be catchin' this summer. Lovely it was." Kieran straightened his back, smiling. "Goin' out tomorrow—6:00 a.m. Come along?"

"Got to broker a horse for a guy. Another time," Jack said, straitening and stretching his back.

"Say, I hear they got the horses doin' flaps—racin' on Geesala beach this mornin'. Got any horses for that?"

"Could have, but no. This deal I am working on is bigger," Jack said, flipping the end of the cigarette into the water. Circles pooled from where it landed, not sinking.

"Aye." Kieran studied the net in his large hands. "Hear they got the relay lads in the Blacksod Point Challenge Triathlon today as well. They'll be takin' up the ocean as we be chattin'—New Yorkers, I hear. Swimmin' all day long between the buoys."

Jack said, "New Yorker's?" He lit another cigarette and threw the match in front of him. It hissed when it hit the water. "You don't say."

"Triathlon swimmers, they are. Three hundred lads are swimmin' in the race. Beautiful swimmers they are, even in rough water." He rubbed his hand over the gray stubble on his chin. "Get up good speed. Manage to survive in Blacksod Bay, they do. Bit of pain 'tis. They got these buoys rigged for safety if they be needin' a rest."

"Real challenge," said Jack, looking around, not seeing the swimmers. "Where are they?"

"Settin' up later for the race. Startin' here at the lighthouse—Blacksod Lighthouse, it is. Over there." He pointed. "See the startin' line markers on the water? Practicin' they are."

"Yeah, but what's all this about?" said Jack.

"Forgot for a second you're a yank," he said, tying a knot in the net. "Blacksod is the furthest point west before you reach America. Lighthouse is in the Guinness *Book of Records*, lad. One of two square lighthouses in the world, they say. That's where the race started and this is where it will begin today."

"What does that have to do with anything?" Jack inhaled, fixed his gaze on the waves sliding in and out along the curved sandy shoreline. Small colorful shacks along the beach lined up like dominos looking out on the bay.

"I'm gettin' to it," he said, as he pulled the netting tight between his teeth, pinching off the loose end. "This place we're sittin' in changed the course of the D-Day landings. Neutral we was—Ireland, that is."

Jack inhaled, waiting, not liking the story. The water looked black under his feet. Kelp grew high, tangling itself in the murky water below him. He could see his shadow, smaller than what he thought of himself.

"The lads were sendin' the original forecast to Churchill from here in 1944. Tellin' him what weather was comin' in across Ireland."

"Good to know," he said and yawned. "I'm feelin' a bit thirsty. Think I'll head up for a pint. See you there."

"Aye, after the mendin' of the last net." He pulled another string in place, tightening the knot.

The crests of water were gray and silver as Jack moved along the beach. Underneath the curl of the waves were dark triangles. He could see the flicker of small fish swimming in circles in the shallow areas as he approached McGinty's Pub, avoiding Carrick's Pub from the night before. It was getting hot, and he was sweating under his shirt.

Entering the pub from the rear, he heard traditional music and smelled yeasty beer, while cigarette smoke fogged the air. An older man sat in the corner, smoking a pipe. Several fishermen huddled at the bar, their cigars contributing to the white haze clouding the room.

Taking a seat at the bar, he ordered a shot of Bushmill's Scotch. Changing his mind, he said to the bartender, "Make it a double, Kevin. And no. I don't want anything to eat."

"Down in the luck, Jack?" asked the bartender, placing the jar in front of him.

"No fish, that's all," he said in a hard voice, downing the drink. "I'll have another."

He felt fine. He knew it was time to buy another horse from Miles Bourke.

TWENTY-SIX
DONEGAL AUCTIONS

S tumbling from McGinty's Pub, Jack got into his dark blue Ford pick-up truck and called Marla on his drive to Donegal Auctions. Weaving back and forth across the dividing line on the road, he said, "Bourke's showing horses today—I'm gonna buy another one for Sheik Abdullah. Wanna meet me there?" Jack frowned at her answer.

"Marla, I told you. I can buy a horse there without a middleman. I am the middleman—what am I thinking?" He laughed at his own joke, feeling good.

She said nothing.

"Where are you anyway? Sounds like a boat horn?" he said, wandering all over the road. She said it was the television at mother's house. Jack said he'd call her later and parked the truck.

The buyers and breeders lined up against the red metal rail of the horse auction block, and he joined them. The shouting and bidding for thoroughbred racehorses had started, and he had to squeeze into a place. Seeing men and women crowded on wood tiered bleachers watching the show made him laugh—suckers. They talked over each other, out bid each other and listened to cell phones, knowing nothing about horses like he did.

The place was alive—men arguing over prices, women crying at the loss of their horses, young boys and girls standing around talking or shoveling after the horses. It did not faze him. He was there for the prize—a big one at that. In the center ring, men paraded horses in a circle in front of the crowd. He watched and waited for the one he wanted. Jack studied his price sheet making calculations. Miles Bourke's horses were next, and the top sellers. He was ready.

The auctioneer rattled off the next horse, "Duke, brother of Rex..."

Jack heard, "Blah, blah, blah." He already knew the specifications of this brother horse to Rex. It was the one he had just sold to Sheik Abdullah, but things had gone wrong. He remembered hearing from Kevin in the bar about the Callaghan brothers. It stirred up his thoughts, made him angry. Those damn idiots hunting on my land, he thought to himself. Shooting my Rex on Bourke's farm. What were they thinking? They ought to be shot themselves—damn fools.

Looking at the brother–in–blood horse Duke gave him an idea. He would substitute this one for the one they killed—the sheik would never know. They looked exactly alike. Sheik Abdullah would never know the difference; he had never seen Rex. The fool Kamal was the loser that brokered the deal with him—he was a complete idiot for a sheik's broker. Yeah, he thought, I will swap horses—it was a perfect plan. He smiled and got ready to bid.

"Who'll give me one million to start the bidding?"

A few men held up their hand to bid. Jack cut in and shouted, "Two million."

The men looked shocked and stopped bidding.

"Sold," the auctioneer said, smacked the gavel, and stopped the bidding. "The next horse…" he went on with the details, but Jack wasn't listening. He had his prize—his substitute.

Dodd, Miles' head man walked up to Jack and said, "What time would it be good for us to be deliverin' this fine horse to you?"

"Never. I'm taking him with me now," Jack said. "My trailer is next to the paddock. Load him up."

"No, we'll be doin' the delivery for you. It's part of the sellin' and the buyin', it is."

"Let me tell you something old man," Jack spat at him. "You won't be delivering anything. This horse is not *Rex*—but he'll have to do. You got my last horse shot. What if somebody put a gun to your head? You gonna go back for more?" he said in an angry voice to Dodd. "No, I'll take him myself from here. Load him up. The door is open. I'll be ready to go in half an hour, so get it done."

"Are you daft? You dint have a horse named Rex. T'was Sheik Abdullah's horse. Don't know where you gettin' that information from, but it's a lie. Was an accident, the shootin' of our Rex, it was. What do you know about it?" Dodd squinted his eyes at Jack.

Jack realized he said too much. "Lucky guess. I hear things. But it doesn't change anything. I'm taking the horse with me." Jack noticed Dodd watching him with narrow eyes.

"Where are you from?" Dodd said, bunching and clenching his fists. "You American?"

"No place you've been," he laughed in his face.

"That so? Ah well, we'll be happy to be deliverin' Duke to the stables tomorrow afternoon. That's what's on the invoice."

"Like I said, no you won't. Take him to my trailer. The blue one parked by the paddock. You can't miss it. I'll be there in half an hour." Jack walked away from the old man with the flushed face, who was shaking his head and kicking dirt.

As he moved through the crowd of people, he thought *this is a gold mine.* I'll substitute Duke for Rex—same bloodline, even looks like him—and make a hefty profit. Abdullah will never know the difference between the two horses. He felt good. I have to tell Marla. I can skim a million off the top of this sale—maybe even the next one. The handler Kamal will never know the difference—what a simpleton.

Jack left the auctioneer area and sauntered over to the post bar past the stables. He needed a drink. He'd have a Scotch there to celebrate, before he drove back to Blacksod Pub. After a few too many drinks, he forgot all about his horse trailer parked in the lot. Drinking and toasting himself was his new objective.

TWENTY-SEVEN
BLACKSOD TO BLACKROCK ISLAND

While Jack drove wildly down the road to Blacksod Pub, without his horse, Miles and Laine left the Sullivan property and flew to the island. Sunrays weaved yellowish-white finger trails over green waves as tailwinds pushed them through the sky. After landing, they walked up the path to the cottage.

"Afternoon to ye both," said Patricia, watering the flowers near the front door. "Be havin' your lunch, we will, but your crew's waitin' to talk to both of you now that you've arrived. They're at the lighthouse." She tipped the green can, sprinkling pink and white geraniums in the window boxes.

"Beautiful flowers, Patricia," said Laine.

"That they are. I'll be takin' some inside from the garden out back. These are for the lookin'. Lunch will be ready half past the hour."

"We won't be late for lunch," said Miles in a light tone, winking at her and walking toward the men.

The sound of buzzing and cutting came from busy construction crews setting up scaffolding around the lighthouse. Eamon approached them as they neared. A burly man by his side eyed them suspiciously. Ruddy-faced workmen with tool belts swinging at their waists gripped circular saws and cut slender planks of wood for the scaffolding. The sun beat down on their backs and sweat rolled from their faces.

"Miles, Ms. Sullivan," Eamon said, "this is your foreman, Murray."

"Nice to meet you, Murray," Laine smiled as she shook a strong, calloused hand.

"Ms. Sullivan, my days workin' with you will be a pleasure." Laine watched the large, smiling man bow to her, sweeping the cap from his thick brown hair. His green eyes burrowed into hers.

Laine said. "I am looking forward to it. How far along are you, Murray?"

"Thirty-five this year, single and available. You?" He gazed intently into her eyes.

Miles laughed at the big man. "How *far* on the lighthouse, Murray. Concentrate on the job. Ms. Sullivan will be here all summer. You'll have to watch out for him, Laine. He's up to no good."

"Oh, that. Thought you meant somethin' else, lass." Murray said not taking his eyes off Laine. "We've finished settin' up the scaffoldin' on the east side of the tower. Now we're workin' on the west side. Cracks in the exterior needin' patchin' and repairin', they do. Worked on tearin' out the lighthouse window. It shows a fine view of the ocean."

"Good. It was a real mess."

"Aye, the Mexican lad Rodriquez is sweepin' it up in the map room. We're needin' an expert to be cleanin' the fireplace, we will. We'll do the framin' of the window later this afternoon. The lad will be cleanin' up the extra debris around the scaffoldin' area outside here today."

"Oh, good. Think I'll take a look. Come on, Miles, Eamon. Nice to meet you Murray." Laine knew he would be trouble and she would have to watch her back. He was a charmer and she wanted to steer clear of him. She wondered when she would have some information for Max, but as of this point she was coming up empty-handed.

The men followed her up the winding stairs into the map room where the Mexican boy Rodriguez was sweeping around the fireplace. Laine observed he was wearing a baseball cap with a bonefish on it pulled down low on his forehead—hard to see his face. What was he hiding, she wondered.

"Hello, you must be Rodriguez. I am Laine Sullivan, your new boss. Like to fish?" Laine said pointing to his cap.

"No speak English," the Mexican boy said, black eyes fixed on her then quickly down on the floor. He turned his back on them, sweeping dirt and old papers into a dustpan. Particles of dust floated through the air as rubbish fell into a cardboard box.

Miles said, "Knows enough English to get by, but really very little. Eamon met him in a harbor pub looking for work. He hired him a few days ago to do odd jobs. Guess he helped out on one of the boats, until they didn't need him anymore."

"He's no trouble. A good worker, he is," said Eamon. Seeing Laine watch dust billow into the room, he said, "We'll be takin' the boxes down to the cove. There are old newspapers and magazines in 'em. Nothin' worth savin'." He sat on the dark oak chair at the end of the refectory table, nestling his cap on his knee, smiling big between his ruddy cheeks.

Miles said, "We'll take them by boat to the dump on the back of the island and burn the rest."

"That we will."

"Still a long way to go," Laine said. "The floors need sanding and staining. Scratches on window frames need filling with wood filler, walls patched—a lot to do, before we paint."

Eamon nodded. "Aye, it'll be a right place to entertain when you finish it, Laine."

Murray, having been silent, moved over closer to Laine. Looking her up and down, he said, "I fancy you'll be dressin' up for entertainin' a party here?"

"Sure. Why not?" she said in a clipped voice. Then turning to Miles, she said, "I ordered the wrought iron chandelier we talked about, matching sconces, and a hand carved mahogany bar—it was in one of the estates they tore apart along the coast not far from here. It will make a big difference in the room."

"What estate, Laine?" Miles asked, but Laine couldn't remember. "I will enjoy entertaining here—add a little mystery to the place."

Murray said, "Rodriguez, finish up and carry the boxes down to the docks? Understand?"

The young man's head popped up when he heard his name. He shrugged his shoulders and slumped on a wood crate, tapping his feet on the floor. He stared at Eamon, ignoring Murray.

Murray said in a hard voice, "I'll be showin' him wot to do. Rodriguez, over here." He pointed to a box and motioned for him to pick it up. The boy did not move off the crate, but only stared at him under the low brimmed cap.

Eamon jumped in, "I'll handle this Murray. You've got better things to do than pick on this young lad."

Laine coughed. "Thanks, Eamon. Murray, can you open the other window, please? It is getting stuffy in here."

"Anythin' for a pretty lady." He shoved up the window to the top of the frame. Glass shattered and flew on the floor. "Don't know me own strength—old window it was." He said in a loud, angry voice. "Rodriguez, clean this up." He took two strides over to the Mexican boy, grabbed a broom, and pushed it into his hands. He directed him to the glass pieces. The Mexican boy slowly stood up. He walked to the window and began sweeping the fragments into the dustpan.

Eamon said, getting up from the chair, "Leave him be, Murray. We'll take care of it."

"Thank you, Rodriguez," said Laine, catching the boy looking at her. She smiled at him, but he ignored her and went back to sweeping. Something was off. She felt it, but could not quite place what it was. She would have to think about it—later. Now she had more important things to do.

"The crew's been workin' all mornin'," said Eamon. "We'll knock off for lunch, then we'll be tidyin' up a bit more later. Callin' it quits for the end of the day at half past five."

"Sounds good," said Laine. She went to the refectory table. She searched among the blueprints. "I'll note this in my schedule. There that does it."

The dark-skinned Mexican boy stiffened and stopped pushing a pile of glass into a cardboard box. He pulled out a pack of cigarettes and a match, watching her from the corner of his eye.

"There's no smoking in here," said Miles who was examining the Maggie McClellan painting of the horse farm and stables above the fireplace. "We need to have this restored, Laine. It is filthy."

"Yes, it is on the list. Maggie is actually a friend of mine. She will work on it as soon as we ship it to her. Mind taking it off the wall? We can crate it and send it out from the mainland as soon as possible."

"Give me a hand, Murray." They lifted the massive McClellan oil painting from the wall, carried it over to the doorway, and leaned it against the door.

The Mexican boy gave Miles a puzzled look. He said nothing and lit up.

Eamon snatched the butt from him, tossed it on the floor, and crushed it with his boot.

"Donna mind him. I'll work with him. Doesn't know all the rules yet, he doesn't. Takes time to learn the ropes, lad," he said to the boy, smiling. Then to Laine, "Murray and I were in the bar havin a drink when I met him. He was lookin' for work, so I hired him without references. Been a good worker, he has. Only been with us a few days, right Murray?"

"Aye, " he said. He looked at the Mexican boy, moved close to him, dropped his voice low, so only he could hear. "Didn't know I was a listenin' to ye talkin' to that yank in the pub, did ye, lad? Be watchin' you I am. Don't be takin' the deal and hookin' up with that dirty bloke. Not in your best interest. I know you're gettin' some of this. I heard you talkin' a bit of English." Murray watched the boy fidgeting, looking at his crushed cigarette, and not at him. "I know you're a understandin' what we're sayin'," he said again in a heavy accented voice. "I heard ye speak in the pub. You don't fool me, you don't."

The Mexican boy's face turned hard and red. He slipped quickly behind Eamon, broom stroking the floor in long, uneven choppy strokes with dust flying in the air.

Giving up his conversation with the boy, Murray directed his attention at Laine, saying, "I'll be cleanin' this up for you, Ms. Laine. Where'd you want the old window frame? Take me a while to get the rest of it out of the wall, it will. It's been here a couple hundred years." He scratched his chin. "It's gonna be quite a job. But," he said smiling at Laine, "we'll be startin' again after the feast Patricia is fixin' for us, we will."

"That would be nice." Then to Miles, she said, "What do you think?"

"Take the rest of the window frame out after we eat." He examined the area of the frame that was cracked. "It's rotted—toss it out, Murray."

"Good," said Laine, retrieving her blueprints and photographs from the refectory table. Her scheduling book fell off the table onto the floor, unnoticed. "I'm starved. Let's do this later."

The Mexican boy swept the rest of the glass pieces into the box, staying away from Murray. He maneuvered himself by the table and grabbed Laine's notebook from the floor, jamming it into the back of his pants. He picked up a box of debris and made his way down the steps ahead of the group.

"I'm goin' to tell the rest of the lads outside workin' wot to do," said Eamon. "Me wife had me fixin' the shutters all mornin', pickin' up the mess in the yard, and bringin' her top soil for the flower boxes. I need a rest now and a good supper. I'll be tellin' the crew time to quit—meet you in the cottage. Come on, Murray. Rodriguez?"

Laine said, "He's gone ahead with a box. Funny, he did know what we wanted." She noticed that uneasy feeling she had in her stomach when things were not on course. She would have to be more observant—watch the little things that could lead her to answers in the mission.

The yard looked orderly as Laine and Miles stepped outside with the men in tow. The sun was directly above them at noon as they left the lighthouse. It felt warm on her skin and she liked the breeze from the ocean.

"I'm going to check the boat before lunch to see how it's riding," said Miles. "Winds picked up. I can see it from the top of the cliff. Want to come?"

"Sure," she said as he smiled at her, "but can we first take a look at the window we're tearing out on the west side of the lighthouse?"

"Be my guest," he said, walking with her.

They rounded the wall of the tower. Laine said, "It will let in the light. I think it will make a big difference."

"Yes, I like the idea. We can see the sunset over the ocean from this side of the tower. Sunrise from the other."

"Yes, that's the plan," Laine said, watching Miles put extra wood pieces in the trash bin near the scaffolding. "They're doing a remarkable job in such a short time."

"They're a meticulous crew. I've worked with them for years. Murray is one of the best. A bit overbearing if you know what I mean, but he gets the job done. The men respect him… and the ladies… well, we'll leave that one for later." He laughed at her look.

"He's harmless."

"That's what you think."

"I'm with you," she smiled at him, liking his strong voice. "Hold on," she said. "I want to step back a few yards and see what it looks like from over there by the trees." She stood off to the side. "Looks good to me."

"Are we done here?" She nodded to him. Within moments, they were looking down the cliff at the boats in the cove.

Miles said, "There's Rodriquez talking with some man I don't know. Looks like he carried down the box of trash down to the dock, too. Thought he didn't understand English."

"Strange. What is he up to?" said Laine, eyeing him suspiciously. Something about the man was familiar to her—oh no—not again. He looked like John. Her insides churned and she ran toward the stone steps. This time he would not get away from her. She would find out the truth.

"Hey, where are you going? He sure is quick for not understanding any English," said Miles.

"I have a bad feeling," shouted Laine, flying down the stairs. "I'll be right back."

"I'm coming with you." Miles charged down the steps after her.

Her insides were churning, while she looked at the tall, thin man under the brimmed fishing cap. He took a roll of bills from his pants pocket, peeled several from it, and jammed the money in the boy's hand. The boy quickly shoved it in the pocket of his jeans and looked around. He saw them descending the stairs. He said something to the man who quickly ran back to the boat and jumped in.

"Hey, you there," shouted Miles. "Hold up. I want to talk to you."

Laine saw the boy hesitate, and looked at Miles. The man shouted to the boy who ran to the boat, untied the line, and scrambled inside. Shoving the curragh away from the dock freed them from the land. The engine kicked in, and they sped away from the cove at top speed.

"You there." Miles said in a loud voice, bounding down the steps to the landing at the bottom. "Come back here."

Rodriguez and the man headed out to sea without a backward glance, ignoring his call.

Miles, hands on hips, said in an angry tone, "I don't like this at all. Rodriguez heard me. What the hell were they up to? Who the hell was that with him?"

"They wanted to get out of here in a hurry that's for sure." Laine remembered the way the man cocked his head as he ran—it was John. But what was he doing with the boy and why was he avoiding her? Her update tonight with Max would be good, yet she was no further from the truth than when she began. Why was John involved in all of this? Why did he fake his death—lie to her? She was getting angry, very angry, and she would use every skill she had to get to the bottom of it. She was no fool and he was not going to make her look like one anymore.

"Laine? Are you okay? You seem distant."

"I'm fine. I'm sure that man heard you—Rodriguez, too. This is all wrong. I am trying to piece it together." She watched them disappear into a small dot on the horizon. She kept the idea it was John to herself. She would have to contact her man on the mainland. See what he could find out. She had the description of the curragh and the boy. It might help them discover the connection. But what was it? Nothing made sense.

"If Patricia wasn't fixing a meal, we'd go after them. There will be time for it later. I'm going to find out who that was and get to the bottom of it. I'm going to put in a call to the harbor and see exactly who that is with Rodriguez. When they show up in Blacksod they'll have a waiting party. Let's go eat." Miles pulled out his cell and called Tommy at the police station. He left a message as they headed up the steps to the top of the cliff,

"Good idea." Laine made a note to herself to remember what she saw. She would call Max that evening when she was alone. Describe the boat, Mexican boy, and tell him John was definitely on the island. Max might be able to help her find out what was going on—it was a long shot, but that's all she had. It was all terrifying, a strangely familiar feeling, and she did not like it. What game was John playing now?

TWENTY-EIGHT

The next day was the second trip in the dark, nearing midnight, when Jack and Marla tucked the curragh under a rock ledge at the mouth of the inlet around the corner from the cove on Blackrock Island. Laine was going no place, except with them. They used their penlights to stumble up the path leading to the cave, hefting a cloth tarp. A sliver of moon hovered overhead in a starless sky. They finally entered the tunnel entrance and took a path leading them to the cave a short distance from the opening. The wind in the cave swooped down from a hole above in the center of the room. There was a fire pit directly below the hole that was filled with half-burned wood and ash.

Marla dropped the tarp from around her shoulders onto the floor, shivering, and said, "Jaysus." Hugging herself, she picked it up again and wrapped it around her. "It's freezin' in here, Jack. Make a fire in this pit, would you?"

"We can't make a fire, they'll see the smoke, dummy. Once we get moving, you'll warm up. You're going with me to get Laine."

"What?"

"We went over all this at the bar, Marla." He patted his pocket, checking for the small bottle of poison she had given him. "It's here," he said, smiling. "Let's go. I can't wait to put this stuff in her tea in that stupid tin she carries around with her everywhere. She'll be dead within days. Won't know what hit her. Good idea, don't you think?"

Marla sat on the stone slab and shook her head. "You're goin' by yourself, Jack. Get this over real quick. I said I'd help you with the boat. I didn't bargain for climbin' through those tunnels again. Last time, the first time, was enough for me. You know the layout now. You do not need me to lead you."

"No way, babe, you have to show me the way. I've only done it once—you know that."

"You're a smart man. You can figure it out." Marla aimed her light around the cave. Bats fluttered from crevices and soared out of the cracks. She ducked, hands protecting her head, and screamed, dropping the tarp. "All right, all right. I'm going. Let's get outta here. Move it."

"Good girl," Jack said, and pointed his light at the exit. "I'll go first. You follow."

"I thought you said you didn't know the way."

"You can be my guide from behind—just so I can protect you."

"Hmmm," she said, crossing her arms, hugging her shivering body. "Fine. Take a right at the first fork."

"Got it," he said, topsiders shuffling on the wet, rocky floor.

"Should have worn boots without heels. Mine have heels on them. I didn't expect this tonight—I don't know what makes me follow your dumb ideas."

He said in a low voice, "Place is slippery. You could get hurt in here.

Watch it."

"Good time to think of it," Marla said in a sharp voice. "Like you even care if I get hurt."

"What?"

"Nothing."

They inched their way through the winding tunnel. At the first bend the walls closed in and narrowed. Jack smacked his head on a low hanging rock, dropping his penlight. It went out.

"Damn," he said. His fingers swept the ground in search of it. Something scuttled across his hand. "What the hell?" When he jumped up, his head hit the ceiling again.

"Ouch, that hurt," he cried again and felt his head. A small lump was forming on his forehead. Blood trickled down his cheek. "Where's that stupid light?"

"You okay?" Marla focused her beam on his face.

"Get that out of my eyes."

"Okay, just looking." She swung the light on the ground. "You're stepping on it."

He stooped to retrieve it. "I'm not alright," he said. Flipping the switch on his light, he found it did not work. "It's broken, damn it."

"Typical." Marla turned her head from him, smiling.

"What did you say?"

"Nothing." She stifled a laugh.

"Marla, knock it off. I've got enough problems." He wiped the blood off his cheek and stared at it. "What the hell? I'm injured."

"You sure are," she said. "It's just a scratch. Let me…"

"Don't," he said, knocking her hand away from his face. "It hurts like a son of a bitch. Let's get this over with. I can't wait to get out of here."

A few moments later, Jack stopped and fumbled around in his jacket pockets.

"What'd you stop for?" Marla played her light around the dark wet rocks. "We've got to keep going."

"I need a cigarette."

"Now?" Marla asked. "You don't have time. The kitchen entrance door is at least another few minutes. You have to get in there to put arsenic in her tea. Like we talked about. I'm not going to stand around in here freezing and watching you smoke, "she said in a hard voice. "Let's go." Marla rubbed her arms, shivering.

"We've got time." He slapped his pockets for his pack of Camels. His hands shook as he lit five matches before they caught, dropping them on the ground.

"What's the matter with you?"

"Nothing." He threw the empty match cover in the air after striking the last match. Inhaling deeply, he leaned against the wet wall of the tunnel. "This place is disgusting. How could you ever play in here as a kid? Weren't you scared to death?"

"No, I liked it. It was fun," she said. "The dark is my friend. It calms me." Rodents scurried over their feet in the beam of Marla's light.

"Rats. Marla, those are rats!" shouted Jack. "Rats the size of small dogs. Maybe you're right. We can think of a new plan instead of poisoning her. We could kidnap her from her bedroom tonight—forget it. Nab her at the shopping mall or something. Let's go—get out of this place. This is getting weirder by the minute."

"Okay, okay. Keep your shirt on. They're gone," Marla said, watching him sweat. She liked it. "Big tough, Jack. We used to try and trap 'em as kids. Played a little game with them after that. Drowned each rat down by the dock... or at least I did." Marla smiled at him.

"Yeah, you liked the dark as a kid. Right. Not. You're full of it." Jack took a last puff and crushed the cigarette beneath his boot. "Shut up, Marla, I've heard enough of your crazy stories for one day. Which way now?"

Marla righted herself and said, "I was putting you on, Jack. Testing you. Seeing what you'd do. Straight ahead. Keep goin'."

"Yeah right. You're a big tease. Let's go. Gimme that." He took her light.

"No, Jack, give it back. I need it."

"Live and learn, baby." He shot the light back and forth along the dark hole leading the way further into the tunnel ahead of him. It widened and smoothed out past a fork to the right. On their left was an alcove he had not noticed before. A candle was melted into a hole in the rock. They crept along, stumbling through the dark passages toward the kitchen.

"How much farther, Marla? We have to be close."

"Ahead on the right. Look for the wooden plank that bolts the door."

"Here it is. Help me lift this bar off the hinges."

They lifted it and set it on the rocky floor.

"Don't be long when you get in the kitchen. They might hear you if you make too much noise."

"It'll only take a minute," he said, inching through the doorway into the kitchen pantry. Ahead of him was another door leading to the kitchen. He eased it open. The door squeaked and he stopped, eyes darting around the room. Silence—no one was there. Jack stepped inside. Marla poked her head around the corner and peered after him. He waved her back, putting his finger to his mouth.

A dim light from the hallway helped him make his way around. He looked for Laine's *Earl Grey* tea tin. *There it is. He knew it.* Fishing the bottle of poison from his pocket, he unscrewed the cap of the arsenic Marla had given him. Tapping a generous amount into the tea tin, he smiled. Next, he placed the lid back on it, and shook the can several times. When he finished, he made certain all was in place. Nothing was left behind. He scanned the floor for footprints he might have left. He did not see any, so he slipped out of the kitchen, into the pantry, then into the tunnel. They bolted the tunnel door shut.

"Let's get out of here," he said, sweat rolling down his face mixing with the dried blood.

"Did you do it?" Marla whispered.

"Piece of cake. Go ahead and get the boat ready."

"What do you mean, go ahead and get the boat ready?"

"What's the problem?"

"What are you going to do? You'll get lost without me to show you the way out."

"Nope," he said grinning. "I'll find my way back. Maybe Laine will show me out."

She laughed. "Get outta here."

"Go on, Marla. I'll wait until I hear Laine in the kitchen. You know we talked about it."

"Then what?"

"Then I grab her. Simple as that."

"No, that's not the plan. You're grabbing her in the tower, dummy, not the kitchen. Poison takes days to kill her—makes her really sick. You can't nab her in the kitchen—too many people will hear. I thought you knew that," Marla said, kissing him on the cheek. "The poison is our backup plan."

"Marla, you're giving me a headache. Yeah, I know that. She's always up before dawn drinking her damn tea. Then she goes to work. The Mexican kid gave me her schedule. She'll go to the tower to start her work for the day. I saw her daily planner." He glanced at his watch. "It's almost time. Get going. I'll meet you at the boat as soon as I can. I'll be bringing her with me." He gave her a peck on the cheek.

Marla laughed. "Okay. I'll meet you back at the boat. Don't forget to gag her after you conk her on the head and knock her out."

"Are you crazy? Think I'm some kind of... forget it. Laine won't know what hit her. Just like we planned. Then we dump her in the ocean, and the sharks will do the rest."

"Right, Jack," Marla said in a soft voice. "She'll drown, too. Like Norbert."

"Yeah," he smiled back at her. Behind the kitchen door, Jack heard pans rattling. "Quiet," he shushed her, and ran into the dark tunnel ahead toward the tower, flashlight bouncing off the walls.

"I can't see," Marla said in a low voice. "I don't have a light. Oh, yes I do." She fumbled for her cell phone and turned on the flashlight. She only had a few bars left and was delighted it worked in the tunnel. As planned, she exited the tunnel, running down the path to the boat. She climbed in and got everything ready—just like they had planned. She grabbed Jack's foul weather jacket from under the seat and slipped it on. Hiding behind a clump of trees, she waited for him to return. If he did not return in an hour, she would go to their plan B.

TWENTY-NINE

At the same time Jack was in the tunnel heading toward the tower, Marla was hiding in the trees, and Laine was waking to delicious smells coming from the cottage kitchen. Glancing at the clock, she saw it was 6:30 a.m. Rising, she walked to the window. The sunrays were deep, dark orange half mooned by a bright yellow light bathing the ocean in a warm glow. It was beautiful, she thought. Her view of the ocean revealed rolling waves lapping the black rock cliffs. She tore herself away from the peacefulness of the new morning sun, dressed and made her way to the kitchen for her routine cup of *Earl Grey* tea and Patricia's homemade breakfast.

"Good morning, Patricia," she said as she entered the kitchen. "You're up early. What smells so good?"

"Mornin' to you. There's brown soda bread comin' out of the oven. You'll have a cuppa tea, won't you?"

"I will." Laine reached for the tin she had left on the counter the night before. "I always bring my own tea with me when I travel," she said, holding up the canister of *Earl Grey.* "It's my favorite. I don't think you can get it in Ireland." She tapped the leaves into a teaspoon strainer while the kettle boiled. "Want some?"

"No thanks, I had me own black tea earlier," Patricia said, ticking off on her fingers, then began setting nine places at the long oak table. "We'll be havin' a bite to eat when the crew gets here this mornin'. Miles and Eamon went to fetch 'em." Smiling, she wiped her hands on her yellowed apron. "You'll be workin' them today, you will."

"I will. I'll wait and eat with them," Laine said, and dipped the strainer into the hot water in her mug. "Right now, I'm going to the tower to get a few things done. I'll be back shortly." She snapped open the tea strainer, dumped the leaves into the waste bin, and set the strainer in the sink. "If they get here soon, please ask Miles to get me."

"Aye," Patricia said, and pulled out a large black skillet from the cupboard. "We'll be startin' our day off right, we will. Got the fry-up ready, I do."

Laine looked quizzical. "What on earth is a fry-up, Patricia?"

"Rashers—that's bacon to you. Sausages. Fried eggs. White puddin'. Toast. Sliced potato and fried tomato."

"Wow!" Laine exclaimed with a laugh. "That's some breakfast."

"It is. A real Irish breakfast. Those lads will be workin' hard, so we feed 'em good." She stirred the pudding in the pot.

"Sounds great." Laine waved as she left. "Okay then, see you later."

She carried the steaming mug of tea down the hall and up the tower stairs to the map room. She placed it on the round table by her briefcase. Even though the sun came in through the window, the room was dark and dim. She turned on the light, needing it to fill the space with warmth.

"What to do first?" She unrolled the blueprints. "Looks like the window today. Knock it out. Make it twice the size. Let some light into this creepy place. What a beautiful sight." She looked out over the Atlantic Ocean.

Waves bounced and rolled as green foamy crests curled over the peaks of jagged water. Ebony storm petrels soared above the waves and flew toward the black rock cliffs. She heard the high pitch of birds singing in the distance. Laine left the window.

Picking up her designs, she said in a loud voice, talking to herself, "We'll get this place looking cheerful in no time." As she reached for her briefcase, her mug of tea crashed to the floor.

"Oh, no." She glanced around the room. "Where is a mop when I need one? Maybe Patricia has one." She ran from the room, spiraling down the staircase, looking for something to clean up the tea.

THIRTY

Jack, hidden above the fireplace in the tunnel, listened from the hatch. It was quiet. *The poison is working,* he decided. He climbed down the niches in the fireplace. The room was *empty. Empty.* He dropped onto the floor, nicking his shin on the grate, and tripping over the andirons. Tumbling into the room, he landed in a puddle of water.

Slapping the seat of his wet pants he said, "What the hell is *this?*" He clamped his mouth shut, fearful someone might have heard. "Where the heck is she? I know I heard her," he said in a low, quiet tone, patting his pants again.

Spying the broken fragments on the floor, he said, "Damn it, she spilled her tea. Now what am I gonna do?" He looked around the room. "Guess it's time to get the hell out of here. The crew will be here shortly."

He kicked a piece of the mug aside and tracked through the puddled tea across the floor as he entered the fireplace. Grabbing a niche in the rocks, he inched his way up the secret entrance back into the tunnel. Slamming the hatch shut, he flipped on the penlight.

Running, stumbling and tripping on the uneven path, he sped down the tunnel, flashlight leading the way. He had to make time to stay ahead of Miles and his crew.

Marla was going to be furious. They'd have to come back again. Or find a new way to get rid of her. This was turning into some kind of joke.

His only thought now was to get off the island. He knew from the Mexican boy Rodriguez that a crew would be coming early that morning, and he was almost out of time. At the first fork he took a left.

Nothing looked familiar.

It took him a few minutes to realize what he had done. He backtracked. He had three choices at the fork: left, right, and center. Choosing center, he proceeded to run down the tunnel with its twists and turns. The ceiling dipped and the tunnel began to narrow as he ran. He smacked his head on the low ceiling for the second time.

"Shee-it," he yelled. "Son of a bitch. Damn rocks." He touched the gash on his forehead and pushed up from the ground in a crouch. "Now what do I do? Should have listened to Marla. We should have left when we saw the rats. *Rats.*" He flung himself from the wet, slippery, rock path and ran bent over down the rest of the passageway.

Water dripped from overhead, letting him know he was in the wrong part of the tunnel.

"Now, I've done it. I'm completely lost," he mumbled in a hard voice. "It smells of stinky, stale air in here—moist, moldy—old. What if I can't find my way out?" His mind unraveled and he whipped around to go back the way he came. Black shadows played tricks on him He was terrified, but he kept from screaming out, and he weaved in and out of the narrow tunnels half bent over, feeling nauseated.

"Can't hear the ocean," he said after taking another wrong turn. He leaned against the wall and caught his breath, thinking. The dampness smelled of stale sewer water.

"What if there are more rats in this part of the tunnel? I'll never get outta here. I could die in here, and no one would know." Sweat beaded on his forehead and ran down under his armpits staining his shirt.

Shining the flashlight down the endless black hole, he backtracked once again for the last time, he hoped. He returned to the spot where the three tunnels merged again. This time, he took the fork to the right.

"This looks familiar," he said in short breaths. He spotted his discarded matches on the ground, and heard the waves. "I did it," he screamed, shutting his mouth as fast as he had opened it. He had found the opening that would lead him outside to fresh air—and no rats. He smelled salt in the air—the ocean. He saw the path and ripped through the forest toward the boat and Marla.

His shirt and pants were wet by the time he flew down the pathway and ran on the shore to the curragh.

Marla was waiting for him in the bow, putting on red lipstick.

"We gotta get out of here. Now!" Jack pushed the boat out into the water, jumped in, and fell half on Marla's lap.

"Ouch, what the hell, Jack? What are you doing? That hurt." She stared at him. "Get off me. You smell. You're getting blood all over my jacket. Look at you—your pants are soaked. *What happened?* Where is Laine?" She straightened herself while he scrambled over her to get to the console. He fumbled under the seat for the key and jammed it in the ignition. The engine caught and they zipped backward out of the inlet.

"The deal is off. Don't ask me any questions."

"What? Where's Laine?" she said in an angry tone. "What's going on?"

"Not now," he said in a hard voice. "Miles' crew will be landing on top of us any minute. We've got to get the hell out of here." He jammed the throttle to its maximum. Marla was thrown about in the small boat, but

Jack did not seem to notice. He hit each wave full force and slammed the hull through them, dodging the spray as it shot over the bow.

"Stop it. You're going to kill us," she said in a loud voice. "Slow down."

He concentrated on steering the boat through the waves and putting distance between himself and the island.

"Talk to me. You brought me all the way over here for nothing?" Marla held tight to the seat after righting herself from the bottom of the boat. "What the hell happened?"

Waves splashed over the bow in a cascade of spray.

"We have to come back. Laine wasn't there."

"Not there? Are you kidding? You kept me awake all night? For nothing?" she screamed, wiping salt water from her eyes. Black mascara streamed down her cheeks and her lopsided red lipstick made her look like a clown.

"Just shut up," he said. "I've had enough of it. She was there, but then she wasn't. That's all I can tell you. We have to come back." The boat pitched and rolled. The bow slammed and thumped against the waves, hull shuddering as it ploughed through the sea.

Marla said, "No way. I'm feeling seasick, Jack. I'm not used to being bounced around like this. My back hurts." Marla said in a heavy voice, tears running down her cheeks.

"Tough. Get used to it," he said in a hard voice.

Marla was silent, watching him grip the wheel and force the boat to take the waves.

The curragh leapt toward the mainland while the spray from the ocean continued to drench them relentlessly.

After a while, Marla shouted, "Jack, we're gonna sink. The boat is filling with water."

"We're not gonna sink," he said in a loud, hard voice. Irritated, he spun the wheel to starboard and then to port to keep the boat on course, slicing through the ten-foot waves. "Hang on or shut up. Do whatever you have to do."

Marla was pale, and her hair hung limp around her face.

"Damn it," he said. "We don't need this."

"We do need it," said Marla. "We have to get rid of her."

"Not that, you dumb cow. There's Miles' boat. He's coming straight at us. Exactly what I wanted to avoid."

"What're we going to do, Jack?"

"Nothing. Pull your hood over your face—quick. Flatten yourself on the deck."

"No way." Marla tried to squeeze herself into a small ball in her seat. "I can't. I'm sick."

"Do it now. He'll see you." He jammed his hat low on his head, crouched behind the wheel, and made himself small.

"Too bad," she said in a weak voice. "Great plan you had."

Jack angled the boat away from Miles. "Yeah, it was a great plan until it got screwed up, alright. Got a new one, Marla?"

"No, but you'll think of one. I know you will." She smiled up at him.

"You bet I will." Jack fixed his eyes on the lighthouse tower at Blacksod Harbor, not looking at her.

As they veered north, going out of their way to miss Miles, he saw the Olympic swimmers ahead, moving through the rough water. Skiffs ran along next to them as they neared the last buoy. Their arms propelled them through the waves like fans spinning on a hot day. Nothing was going to stop them from finishing their trial workout. Nothing.

Jack admired that. He felt he was one of them. Going forward, moving fast in the waves, guiding his curragh against all odds—against Miles and his crew. Against Laine—yes, against her—that was the goal. He would have to try again. Men riding wave runners jetted about the ocean towing sled-like boards behind them to rescue tired swimmers.

Rescue them—not let them drown like he would do to Laine.

"How can they swim in these waves?" Marla said.

"They are strong. Work out all the time for many years. They also have on wet suits to make them float along like a life jackets. They train hard for this race in swimming pools that blast tons of water against them while they swim. Yesterday, the team leaders put out extra buoys to guide them for the competition. There is one close to Blacksod Harbor. We are heading there now. I've been reading up on them."

"What are you talking about?"

"Nothing, Marla. Nothing. Nothing for you to worry about."

A new plan was forming in his mind while he watched the swimmers. Yes, he thought, that's how we'll do it. We will use the cave to hide Laine, if their plans get sidetracked again. Yes, Marla's cave where she hid from Miles when they were young. She will love it. Why didn't he think of it sooner?

"I'm cold," she said in a loud, whiney voice.

"It's not far. Hang on." He saw Marla wince as the boat pounded on the next wave.

"I've got a new plan. One I know you will really like."

"I bet you do," she said, giving him a hard stare.

Clouds covered the sun and the wind tore through the sea creating gigantic waves around them. The curragh was sturdy and it bobbed through the water. Jack steered clear of hundreds of Olympic swimming competitors in black wetsuits, breast stroking against the current and the waves as they headed for Blacksod.

THIRTY-ONE

While Jack and Marla sped away from the island in the curragh, Laine ran from the tower and flung open the door to the mudroom, looking for something to mop up her spilled tea. She dug through buckets and rags, stringy mops, and other paraphernalia, searching for a broom to clean up the pieces.

"Ah, here's one, "she said, producing a broom and grabbing the dust pan. She was blocked by Murray hanging up his foul weather gear when she turned to leave. The rest of the workmen trailed into the kitchen to have breakfast and did not stop to ask what she was doing.

"Good morning to you, Miss Sullivan. You're up early—a lovely lass you are this time of day. Need a helpin' hand with those, you do? I'm good for that—with the hands, that is, I am," he said, eyeing her with a grin as she backed up from him.

"No, Murray, I can take care of this myself. Have you seen Miles?" She shoved the broom and dustpan in front of her. "Can you please step aside?" She tried to move past him, but he stepped in front of her. She did not want to use force, so she played the game.

"You're the only one I see," he said in a gentle voice. "Lovely sight you are on such a fine day. Like a red rose on a summer mornin', you are," he said in a deep voice.

She looked up into his eyes. In a friendly tone, she said, "You're a charmer, Mr. Murray. Move it. I have things to do. Now, please," she nudged him out of the way. His eyes moved up and down her body. She quickly pushed him out of her way.

"Morning, Laine." Miles said, coming into the mudroom as Murray stumbled backward. "Is there a problem?" He focused his eyes on Murray.

"No problem," she said in a strong voice. "I broke a cup in the tower. Murray came in and offered to help."

"Likes me she does—any man can see that, he can." Murray laughed and stepped aside.

Laine scooted around him.

"Murray, you're full of yourself. I think Patricia's waiting on breakfast for all of us," said Miles.

"Well, then, it will have to be later, Miss Sullivan—the helpin' you clean up that is." He gave her a wink. "Lovely lass, she is, Miles, won't you be agreein'?"

"Yes, she is. You and your men will be putting in a long day today. Patricia is waiting." He smacked a friendly pat on his back. "Go get some breakfast, man."

Murray said in a hearty voice, "That I will. Didn't want to leave Miss Sullivan in her troubled state, did I, when she be needin' a *man* to do the job?" Flexing the muscles on his arms, he smiled.

Miles said in a friendly tone, "I don't think you were thinking about cleaning up, Murray. I know you well."

"That you do, Miles. Especially when there's a lovely lass as this needin' my help, she does." He squared his massive shoulders and left them,

Miles took the supplies from her. "Watch out for him, Laine. He's got his heart set on you."

"He's a handful, Miles, but harmless. A big flirt," she smiled at him. "Not afraid to say his feelings—that's for sure. It's refreshing in a way."

"Don't know about that," Mile said in a defensive tone. "Usually gets what he wants from the women. Has a reputation and a string of lasses in every town. I wouldn't let your guard down with him around—unless you want to, that is," Miles said in an edgy tone.

"Hadn't thought about it in that way. Something to think about," she said in a teasing voice and laughed when she saw the look on his face, liking it. "I need to pick up my broken mug on the map room floor," she said in a light voice. "Not a big job. I should really…"

"Can't it wait until after breakfast? Isn't there something you want to talk about?"

"Yes, but we can talk later," she said, catching herself.

"How about talking now?"

"I need more time to think it through. There have been a lot of coincidences, since I got here. Too many things don't add up. First, I thought I saw my husband in town. Next, you show me the land I never knew about, and then Rex, and the voice in the tower."

"What voice?"

As quickly as she could she related her experience earlier that morning.

"I have an odd feeling I'm being watched. I know it sounds silly, but I heard my name being called." She wanted to draw him into her confidence. Maybe he would confide in her about the problems with the horses.

"That would make a difference. That old tower gives off some queer noises."

You're right, it does. But then again, there are some strange things going on around here." Laine had the same bad feeling before in Cuba right before they abducted her—a sixth sense. Max had told her early this morning during their phone call to trust her instincts. Watch your back—don't trust anyone—not even Miles. She reached for the small pistol hidden in the back of her jeans under her shirt. Needed to feel it there to comfort her—remind herself she could use it if she had to.

"Let's enjoy the 'frying up,'" she said. "It's all so silly."

"Yes, let's. I'm glad we talked this over."

"Me too." Murray was the least of her problems.

THIRTY-TWO

They finished the breakfast and returned to the map room in the tower. The construction crew worked under Murray's direction on the exterior of the tower. Miles and Laine were inside going over the blueprints.

Crash! A clattering and scraping noise came from outside the open window. Miles and Laine ran to the window, searching each other's faces, puzzled.

"What was that?" she asked as she ran to the open window, peering down. "The scaffold has collapsed."

"Follow me down the steps," said Miles, taking her hand. "It's not safe."

They descended the winding staircase to the base of the lighthouse and exited through the door. Picking their way through the rubble, they found metal poles bent and twisted from the collapse.

"There's a gash running from the east tower window to the base of the lighthouse," said Laine in a low voice.

"This is a disaster," said Miles in a hard voice. "Anyone hurt?"

The men were hurriedly pulling wood planks from one area of the debris. "Aye, hurry," said one of the crewmen to the group of men working on the site. "He doesn't have long. The weight will crush him to death."

"Eamon, what happened?" Miles said in a loud voice. "Who is under the scaffolding?"

"It's Murray."

"Oh no," she said in an anxious voice. Laine saw his legs bent backward at an unnatural angle. "Quick, get him out of there."

"Be quick about it, lads," said Miles in a commanding voice. He elbowed his way through the planks and yanked up board after board to help free Murray, who was pinned underneath the weight.

"Aye, poor bloke," Eamon said in an anxious tone, lifting the end of a board that had fallen on Murray's torso. Sean took the other end and they lifted it from his body.

"His hand moved. For the luv of… he's alive," screamed one of the men.

The men worked faster, tossing wood and metal behind them as they freed his body.

Miles shouted. "Hold on, Murray. We'll get you out of this. Hold on."

In a short time, Laine watched the men free him from under a tent of wood and steel. He was deathly pale and she knew she was going to blow her cover if she was not careful. Her training would help to save his life. She made her decision.

"Take it easy, Murray, we'll get you to the hospital," said Miles.

"Murray, no worries," Eamon said close to his ear. "Hang in there, lad."

"Let me see him. I'm trained in this kind of thing." Miles' surprised look gave her cause, but she dismissed it. Taking his wrist and applying pressure, she said, "He's got a pulse. But barely." She felt his arm. "It's broken. I need something to stop the bleeding here on his arm. Miles, give me your shirt."

He gave it to her.

She ripped it. Wrapping the strip around his arm helped to apply pressure to stop the bleeding. "He needs medical attention—now. We have to get him to the hospital. We need to make a stretcher to evacuate him out of here. Let's get moving. There's no time to waste."

"I'll get the helicopter ready. Men, put together a makeshift stretcher. Hurry," Miles said to his men. "Do what she tells you." He left them.

The crew did as he instructed. They carefully lifted Murray onto the stretcher per Laine's instruction. Now they were carrying him across the lawn toward the helicopter.

The wind from the rotors tore at them as they got closer. Dirt flew in the air and they covered Murray with a tarp. They moved swiftly toward the helicopter.

THIRTY-THREE

The men carried Murray to the open door of the helicopter, strapping the stretcher down in the rear compartment. Laine and Eamon climbed aboard. The door barely closed when Miles lifted off the tarmac. Thump, thump, thump the rotors beat the air as they flew toward Donegal Airport. Miles expertly controlled the cyclic stick between his legs, tilting it forward and back to alter the rotors. He maintained his speed and manipulated the collective and the foot pedals. Donegal was in view in a short time.

Laine said in a gentle tone to Murray, "Stay awake, big guy. We're almost there. Don't fall asleep on me."

A slight grin curled from the corner of his mouth. His eyes were reduced to pinpoints.

Blood soaked his chest where his right arm was cocked at an awkward angle. His jeans were stained with blood on both legs. Watching him,

Laine knew he was in shock.

"Murray, stay awake," she said in a loud voice. He blinked them open. "Look at me. I need you to stay awake."

His eyes squinted at her, forcing them open, staring at her. "Miles, danger is a comin'. Jack and Mexican boy. Watch out." He drifted off.

Laine puzzled over his comments. It did not add up. She wondered how Murray was a part of all of this.

"Murray, you're one tough man." She talked to him in a soft voice. "Keep your eyes open—on me, Murray— look at me. Try to stay awake."

Murray stirred and groaned. "Jack—Rex— Miles." Opening his eyes, shutting them, opening them again—breathing hard in a low tone, trying to focus on Laine. "Tellin' the boy. Miles. Eamon…"

"He wants to talk to you, Eamon."

Eamon put his ear near him. "He's sayin' Jack in Donahue's Pub—the boy. Can't make out the rest."

Murray grabbed his sleeve with his good hand, pulling him down. Murray said in a whisper, "Ach, bad horse business, drugs—Mexican boy. Rodrig…" His voice trailed off.

He turned to Laine, shrugged. "Hard to be understandin' him. But somethin' off."

This caught Laine's attention. "Murray—good—we are here for you. We can talk about it later," she said. "Save your breath and keep your eyes on me." She watched him struggle to keep his eyes open keep his eyes open.

"I've information—tell Miles." A surge of pain went through him and he groaned, squeezing his eyes shut.

"Hang in there. There'll be time to tell us later, lad," Eamon said.

She leaned near his ear, saying in a soft voice, "Stay with me. I heard you. Miles, the Mexican boy, Donahue's Pub. Rex. I got it. Don't worry, I will tell Miles. We're almost at the hospital."

Bouncing through the sky, the helicopter swung left and dipped as they neared the landing pad.

"I'll ride with Murray to the hospital," said Miles. "The ambulance is waiting. We have clearance to land."

"Got the helicopter ride you been waitin' for—a bit earlier than expected." Eamon grinned at the man. "Hang in there. We're a landin', now. Get you fixed up quick, we will."

Murray mumbled in a raspy voice, "I ..." He tried to talk, but the words failed him as another wave of pain shot through his body. He twisted and struggled to breathe.

"Take deep breaths and try to relax," said Laine, reaching for his good hand. "I know it's bad."

"Aye," he said watching her, forcing himself to lay flat, blood soaking the stretcher.

"Murray, we'll be finishin' the talk later—hear you had quite the time with the lasses in Donahue's Pub last eve." He winked at Laine, wiping the sweat from his forehead with his shirt sleeve. "Hold on there, lad, it's a bugger it is."

"Yes, we all can't wait to hear what you were up to," said Laine in a soft tone, smiling at him. "You're my favorite foreman. Hear the ladies were standing in line." She saw him smile back at her. "No one is taking my foreman's spot. I'm counting on you to get better. Need you to do that for me, Murray—I know you can do it."

Miles dropped the helicopter down.

"We will be at the hospital with you. I will personally check up on you."

Murray struggled again, smiled a small smile, and bit on his lower lip, fighting back the pain sweeping through his body. She could see he was slipping out of consciousness.

"We're here. Hold on."

THIRTY-FOUR

A short time later in Donegal Hospital's waiting room, Eamon went for coffee and Laine listened to Miles on the cell phone with his police cousin Tom.

He was saying, "The scaffolding let go on the lighthouse tower. Murray was critically injured. We're at the hospital." He waited for a response, listening. "Check it. Nothing like this has ever happened before. That Mexican boy Rodriguez didn't show up for work this afternoon. He was helping to secure the bolts yesterday on the scaffolding."

Laine looked over at him. She could see his face muscles tighten.

"Never picked up his check. He and Murray didn't get along. I saw the boy take off in a boat with some man who paid him money down by my dock. I didn't know the man. I'll tell you the rest later." He hung up.

Laine was watching him. She saw the dark look on his face. "Want to talk about it? It was in her training to be suspicious—alert. Clearly it was sabotage, according to what she saw. Miles had told the policeman on the cell the same thing.

"We're looking for the Mexican boy Rodriquez. I called Dodd at the farm, but they haven't been able to locate him either. Cleared out his bunk—took all his things."

"Who would want to do this to you, Miles?" She thought she would ask the men a few questions when they got back to the island—dig a little deeper. Get Max involved. Murray's incident put this on the top of the priority list for her. She could contact her man here in Donegal and put the word out. Maybe he could get some information from the locals.

"Don't know, but I am going to find out. I put Wilfrid and Tom, my cousins—the garda (police) on it. You met them at the stables the day Rex was shot. They are good at what they do. They'll get to the bottom of it."

"Yes, I remember them," she said. This had to go into her report to Max. "Murray tried to tell Eamon and me something he heard in Donahue's Pub." She told him what he said. "He might have overheard something that could be helpful."

"Yes, you could be right. When he's able, I'll talk to him," said Miles in a cold voice.

"The only time the crew was not together was at breakfast. You and I saw Rodriguez leave the island with the man down by the cove. Laine, giving that boy money might have been a payoff to hurt Murray. It adds up in a certain way."

"Payoff?" she asked, not wanting to give herself away. She had seen it, too. The boy was involved in something with the man. She couldn't make the connection. Listen. That's all she had to do.

"Yes, money. It's too coincidental. Murray is injured—that boy could have tampered with the scaffolding. Who knows? Murray would never have left anything loose. I know his work—been the best foreman for years—conscientious to a fault. It was deliberate all right, but I haven't figured out why."

"Who would want to hurt you or your men?" Laine asked in a soft tone, drawing suspicion away from herself.

"None that I can think of—unless, of course, the Sheik Abdullah's broker has a problem with Rex's death. I told him we would replace Rex with his brother —same quality—they even look exactly alike. He was irate and threatened to sue me. He finally settled for Duke at half the price. I gave him the other half of the money back, so he shouldn't have been out of sorts. He got the best deal and I lost my best horse and his brother-in-blood horse."

"Seems like more than fair," said Laine, memorizing what he was telling her.

"And well, yes, there was another incident a few months ago. We sold a horse to the same broker. He sold that one to the sheik, but it died on the track. But we had nothing to do with it. The vet called it a 'milkshaking' incident at the Kentucky Derby. Doesn't seem feasible the broker would seek revenge for it—unless of course, he caused it. That crossed my mind, but to what gain? He already made his money from the sale."

Laine thought for a moment before answering, "I don't know how he thinks, Miles. I'm sure you gave him another excellent horse. It does seem strange. What is 'milkshaking'?"

"They inject the horse to make it go faster—like a protein shot up the nose. I can show you the literature I have at the lighthouse. It is completely illegal. What a fiasco that was. The horse died on the track and they tried to blame me."

"It sounds awful. I read something about it in the States. You were exonerated. I'd like to read the information on it," she said in a quiet voice. This was her ticket inside. Miles would give her the information first hand. She might get a break after all.

"Yes, I was not at fault, but it nearly ruined my business. The sheik is still buying from me, so I guess we'll see how it goes in the future. I sold Duke to him today. I have several, but Rex was the best. He got Duke, my second best, this afternoon while we were at the hospital. Dodd took care of it. We told him we were going to deliver the horse to him, but he didn't want that. There was some kind of mix-up at the auction. He demanded that he take the horse straight from there, but he never showed up to load the horse in his trailer. Odd American man, from what Dodd says. He thinks he got drunk and forgot to get him. Crazy business."

"He was an American?" She was getting at the heart of the matter. Keep him talking, she thought. "Forgot to pick up his racehorse? Sounds like a whack job to me."

"Yes, it was odd. There was a big change of plans a few hours ago. The sheik's headman, Kamal, came from his farm and picked Duke up in Sheik Abdullah's private horse trailer—today—a few hours ago. It was arranged for tomorrow with the broker, but the sheik wanted him sooner. From what I heard, the horse trailer had Sheik Abdullah's name on the sides in solid gold letters and diamonds. My men at the farm were flabbergasted when it rolled up to the stables all shining and white. There was a line of armored cars in front and in back of it. The men at the farm have never seen armed guards wearing bulletproof vests in military vehicles before to pick up a racehorse—a lot of security for one horse. Seems unnecessary. The horse is insured. Funny thing—they sent his headman, not the usual broker, to get him. No broker fee this time."

Laine said, "Over the top. But then, I'm not in the sheik's position to buy a thoroughbred racehorse of any kind, let alone send a fancy rig to pick him up." Things were not adding up. This was way out of line. Something was happening with the sheik's horses and the American broker. Even by Miles' own admission, there was a death on the track surrounding the last horse he sold to the sheik at the Kentucky Derby. The whole thing smelled funny. Laine had to reach Max before tonight and relay what she had heard as soon as possible—things were escalating. The sheik had changed tactics for picking up his horses and handling the money—where was it really going? Who was this other broker? She would have to ask Miles about him in a way that seemed like she was not prying.

"It's odd the sheik wanted to cut out the broker," she said. "I'm sure he'll be furious."

"I would think so. That's essentially what the sheik did today by cutting him out. No commission was written in the revised contract he brought with him. There is no broker, or anyone in place in the future for that matter, per Dodd. We've never had a problem before—hate to have one now. I have to deal directly with Sheik Abdullah, or whomever he sends to do his bidding. I've never done business like this."

"Is it different from before?"

"Yes, there was always a broker for the sheik. The same one bought the last two horses and Rex."

"And the men picked the horse up in a golden carriage," she laughed. "What a sight to see. Wish we were there," she said in a light voice.

"I guess. Nothing about it rings true. That's not what we do. We like to personally deliver our horses to the client, especially the clients who live here in Ireland. It is our philosophy to make sure the horses are safely transported to their owners. It's protocol, and our insurance covers it in case something happens."

"That does seem odd, given it's the way you've been doing business in the past. Surely the sheik knows that."

"We've done it that way for years without a glitch. He knows it. Possibly the new broker wasn't working out, so he let him go. What was his name?" he stopped, trying to remember. "I had Dodd deal with him, so I don't' recall who it was."

"You can hear what he says when we get back. Maybe he found out something about the new man and the drunk American."

"Oh well, I'm not even going to try to get it straight. Oddly enough, sending his own man Kamal was unprecedented. Dodd told the broker he'd have to wait until tomorrow to get the horse, but that went sideways. He started screaming and yelling in the paddock, said the sheik would be so mad he would buy up all my land and turn it into a chicken farm."

She saw him hesitate, glancing at his watch.

"He was out of control for a while until Dodd calmed him down. If I were there, I would have thrown him and his men off the property—sale or no sale. Who these people think they are is pretty amazing. Just because they have lots of money does not give them the right to put down and belittle other people. That's my feeling on the subject, anyway. When we get back to the farm, I'll show you the surveillance camera tapes. Would you like that? Keep it interesting while you're here." He looked hard at her and did not smile.

"Yes, I would. The sheik sounds impatient," she said in a cold voice, giving him a cold look. "Learned a little something about the horse racing business of buying and selling. So there's that. Do you have tapes of the American that bought your horses?"

"Yes, I do. We have the tapes of everyone who buys our horses. It's a precautionary measure. A lot of politics are involved. Big money in his horses, especially on the international scene. With the trouble at the Kentucky Derby, I should be happy the sheik and his friends are still buying from me. There's a lot of money laundering floating around the race track and I don't want to get involved in it. I run a clean-cut business, so I like to keep the clients I have. I know each of them personally."

"Do you know anything about the money laundering that takes place in the States?"

"No, you're my first insight into that kind of trouble." She felt uneasy.

"I sold the sheik a horse that someone drugged or injected—called it 'milkshaking'—at the Derby. Horse died on the track during the race. I had nothing to do with it. It's being investigated. The sheik is demanding the White House get involved."

"The President?" Laine's voice was calm. She needed more information.

"Afraid so, the sheik is demanding compensation for the loss of his horse on U.S. soil—besides wanting to sue me. Saudi royals and their friends may pull out of the racing business and set up their own races. A lot of money is tied up in this. It'll hurt the sport and make the U.S. look foolish. On a personal level, it could ruin me."

"I had no idea," said Laine in a soft voice. "This is huge. I hope he is happy with Duke as a replacement for Rex."

"That's what I am hoping. It's not a good situation. I meet with him next week on the island to smooth things out. He entered Rex in one of the richest turf races there is in France next month. The Prix de L'Arc de Triomphe at the Longchamp Racecourse. He is a Group 1 horse, and he had the best chance of winning the purse. It's 865,000 euros this year. I don't have another champion like him—Duke doesn't even qualify for a 2,400 meter race."

"You've got my attention. Someone had a motive for doing it."

"That's how I feel about it myself. I explained the problem to Kamal—told him Rex was accidently shot. He was extremely agitated. Told me not to worry the sheik about this. He said not to upset him at all. He'd handle it. I told him Duke is the same bloodline, even looks like him. I am going to discuss it with Sheik Abdullah when I see him. You can meet him if you would like to."

"Yes, that would be nice," she said. "They say not to worry, but you have a lot to worry about."

"Too many worries."

"You have your work cut out for you."

"I want to keep the channels open with the sheik. We're friends on a personal level. We attend the same parties and have lots of mutual friends. The problem has to be solved."

Laine said, "I understand." She wanted to keep him talking. He was giving her the intel she did not have and Max would be elated. She would excuse herself and call Max when she got the chance. She could not wait until tonight. This was the link she was searching for to help them move forward.

"I am not sure what he had in store for Rex, but I think it was bigger than we all imagined. He was a winner—there is no doubt about that. Duke will be, too, in his own way. Like I said, they have the same breeding."

"Hopefully, you'll be able to give him what he wants in Duke."

Miles hesitated before speaking. He said, "Kamal told Dodd he would contact the broker himself—tell him he was picking him up. I racked my brain for anything that might be off, but I'm coming up empty. Very odd."

"There are a lot of odd things going on around here. Eamon and I heard Murray warning you to beware of the man in Carrick's Pub. He said Donahue's but Eamon said it was Carrick's place where he hired the boy."

"You say Murray said the man's name was Jack that he had trouble with?"

"Yes, Eamon and I heard him clearly," she said in a soft voice. "It seems I've brought you bad luck. Ever since I've arrived, accidents—or whatever you want to call them—are becoming a daily thing." She added a soft voice to throw him off. She did not want him thinking she was too involved. That name, Jack, kept coming up—here again today.

She wondered what connection he had with Miles?

"I have no idea what's going on," Miles said. "I don't know a Jack. I didn't recognize the man in the cove either—now that I think of it. Another unknown. Now that I look back, I should have gone after him and Rodriguez. Find out what they were doing on the island. I heard from my cousins. They said they didn't come into the harbor that day. They had to land some place along the shore. Another mystery."

"Did you recognize the boat?"

"No—curraghs are common around here. No telling where it came from. There was no name on it I could see. I'd recognize the man's shape, if I saw him again. Could you?"

"I didn't really get a good look at him," Laine said, thinking about the man, thinking about Murrary's information on Jack—thinking about John. She felt angry and had to control it.

Eamon entered the glassed-in waiting room with their coffees. "Hot enough," he said, setting the cardboard box on the small table, then he sat on a plastic chair.

Miles and Laine picked up their coffee with thanks. Laine flipped through magazines, Eamon nodded off, and Miles spoke on his cell for a short time.

"You were an expert with Murray—back there on the island," said Miles, hanging up. "A bit of a surprise how easily you took over. I can tell you've done it before, and it may have saved Murray's life. We're grateful to you, Laine." He smiled at her, then sipped out of the Styrofoam cup.

"I guess I am quick on my feet," she said. Her cell phone rang. Checking the caller ID, she did not answer it, knowing it was Max. "My office. I'll call back later." She muted the ring and slipped it in her pocket.

"Do you have any formal medical training?"

"No," she hated lying to him, but she had to maintain her cover. "None, really. I volunteered with the Red Cross for a short time." Laine stared at his strong face, liking it. "Nothing special."

Miles' forehead creased. "Special enough."

"If you'll excuse me, I need to go to the ladies room." She left the room.

Now inside it, she checked the stalls. Empty. She dialed Max and relayed the information to him as quickly as she could.

"Contact Shamus and tell him to go to Carrick's Pub and find out about the Mexican boy Rodriguez and an American named Jack," she said in a low voice. She relayed details on the broker business problem at Miles' farm, the "milkshaking" incident, and the meeting with Sheik Abdullah next week on the island. She hung up knowing he would follow up on all her intel.

When Laine returned to the waiting room, the doctor was updating Miles and Eamon on Murray's progress. It saved Laine from answering any more questions from Miles.

THIRTY-FIVE
KOOLMORRE STABLES

While Miles flew to the island with Laine and Eamon, the sheik's entourage was busy on his farm. After leaving Miles' stables, the white, shining, gold and diamond caravan rolled into the county of Waterford, several hours from County Mayo ahead of the sheik.

The sun was high in the cloudless sky.

Close to half an hour later, several sleek, black limousines preceded Sheik Abdullah as he rolled into Koolmorre Stables in his Silver Cloud Rolls. Several followed. The entourage screeched to a halt at the stable doors. Sheik Abdullah stepped from his car, and armed guards raced to surround him. His billowing white robes spun and floated across the yard under his long strides over the immaculate paved road. The property was pristine and the horse stables gleamed.

"Wait here," he said to the armed military men at his heels. Motioning for his bodyguard to follow, they disappeared inside. Several guards took their positions on either side of the stable doors, machine guns at the ready. Several other soldiers set up a perimeter along the white fences surrounding the property. They stood at attention, alert behind dark *Oakleys*, guns cradled across their chests—watching, waiting for the unexpected.

Entering the stables, the sheik and his bodyguard removed their sandals, placing them on the mat. Sheik Abdullah stopped and surveyed his stables and the workers.

A long, white marble hallway separated the horse stalls on the left and right. Each gold-barred stall door was polished to a glassy mirror-like finish. Diamond studded names, set in solid gold plates, were fastened on the front of each horse's stall. Hay was covered in parallel lines on the floor and horse dung was removed as fast as it appeared. The palace-type stables were adorned with multiple crystal chandeliers, gleaming brightly from the ceiling.

A line of stable hands, dressed in white uniforms and turbans, were bent—head over their knees—foreheads pressed onto the floor as he passed. All eyes were averted. There was no talking.

"Kamal," the Sheik Abdullah said in a loud voice. His voice boomed and bounced off the cold walls, echoing in the large space.

"Yes, my brother. I am here," said a voice behind the sheik, coming out of a stall.

A short man with a strange dark face, a pointed nose, and a head covered with wrinkles and scars, ran to him. His black eyes peered out from a head wrapped in layers of white cloth and fixed upon the sheik. He lowered them immediately and dropped to his knees, his bare feet pressing into the marble floor. He bowed again and again before the sheik. His thinly pointed, beard-studded face made him appear old before the middle-aged sheik.

"My brother, I am so happy to see you. Assalamo Alaikum," he said welcoming him, grasping the sheik's outstretched right hand, while on his knees, not looking up. He stood as the sheik pulled him to his feet, and the short man kissed the sheik on both of his cheeks welcoming him. "Kaif hal ak."

"Don't offer me peace. Bring me my new horse, Kamal." The sheik looked him over, thrust his hand from his, and waved him away.

"Yes, my brother," Kamal said and shook his head up and down, backing away. To a young-faced groomsman, he said in an anxious tone, "Hurray, bring him out." He motioned to the stall he had come from a few moments before.

All the groomsmen lining the long marble hallway between the stables continued bowing over and over, heads touching the floor, silent.

"Stop," Sheik Abdullah commanded. "Rise and go about your duties." The men scattered to do his biding, in fear for their lives.

Inspecting each of the horse stalls, he floated down the plush red carpet lining the floor. Stopping, examining every detail, he proceeded to the place where his new horse would be brought to him. It was in the center of the white and gray marble room at the end of the hall. His fingers traced the word "Rex" on the gold plate on the horse's stall. He traced it, staring at the letters. Ropes made of gold twine hung on clips and were used to hold the horse in place. The roping design was exquisite and laced with purple threads tightly-woven among the golden material.

In a loud voice, Sheik Abdullah said, "Bring out my new horse to me. Don't keep me waiting, Kamal."

"Here he is, my brother." The man in the pointed beard bent at the waist, bowing low. "Here is Rex. A spectacular racehorse. He will win them all."

The groomer came forward holding the reins of an Arabian horse. Kamal took them and put the horse's nose through the loop of the nose twitch, running his hand up and down the horse's neck to quiet him. They fastened the gold ropes to keep him in place.

"You have inspected him, Kamal?" Sheik Abdullah peered down at the little man. "Is he healthy?"

"Yes, my brother. Yes, he is a healthy, fine horse. I have inspected him over and over myself. Excellent horse. He will make good money for you on the racetrack—a winner." He backed away from the sheik, bowing, giving him more room for his own inspection.

The sheik ran his hands down the horse's legs, along his flanks, and over his forehead. He examined the pasterns and fetlocks, lifted each hoof. His practiced fingers probed the throat and jaw, curled down the lips, tugged up the eyelids. The horse's nostrils flared. He pulled back the horse's lip again, silently reading the numbers tattooed inside.

"What is *this*, Kamal? This is not the horse I bought. Who is responsible for this?" The sheik stamped his feet several times and flung his arms wildly. His white robes billowed around him. Spit flew from his mouth. "Explain this, Kamal." The horse snorted, and bucked, nearly kicking a man close by him.

"But... my brother... you picked out this horse yourself. It is Rex. Rex. You bought Rex from the broker Jack Lafferty at the auction. I picked him up today at Bourke's farm." He petted the horse, talked to him, tried to stop the skittishness, but was not rewarded—the horse bucked and kicked again.

The moment the words left his lips, the sheik struck him across the face. Grabbing the man by the front of his robes, he lifted him off the ground and threw him on the floor like a ragdoll. "Do not tell me this. What numbers are branded in his mouth?" He kicked the man into the horse. "Read them to me." The men kept the horse in place as he jumped, pulling on the gold ropes.

The man rose, cowered before him, and pulled back the lip. He said in

164

a soft voice, "5552140963, my brother."

"Read it again." The sheik grabbed Kamal's throat as he gurgled out the numbers.

"Exactly. Rex has a '7' in his mouth—not a '9'—you blithering imbecile." Letting go of his throat, he pushed him into the horse. The horse threw his head back. The ropes kept him from rearing up on his hind legs. He bucked again, swung his hind legs to the left, and knocked a groomsman to the ground. "Get this nag out of my sight."

"Take him. Remove him," Kamal said in a loud, shaking voice to the closest stable hand. Throwing his hands in the air, he said in a louder voice, "Dispose of him. Now."

"It is you who will be *disposed of,*" the sheik said in a strong voice, looking down at Kamal with dark eyes.

"Give me a chance to find the man Jack who did this, my brother. I will find him, my brother. I will kill him, my brother." He fell to his knees, bowing low, making himself small at the feet of the sheik. Forehead pressing into the marble, begging. It was an unpleasant sight. The man stiffened, waited for the strike.

The sheik stamped his foot onto the man's back. A bone cracked. "Find the horse I paid for by the end of the day, or it will be you who pays with your life." He nodded to his guard, and he removed his foot after another stomp.

Gliding down the carpet, he stopped for his guard to fasten his sandals, before exiting the building. "I will expect you at my suite at 9:00 this evening. You *will* bring *Rex* to me."

"Yes, my brother. Yes, my brother," Kamal said in an anxious, pained voice, tears running down his cheeks. He continued bowing over and over again, bent, in an awkward state. The sheik did not turn, but gave him his back. "I will do as you command, my brother," he choked out the words, "I will seek revenge for you on this day. I will bring Rex to you."

"You will or you will be with Allah today." His fisted hands shot toward the sky.

Sheik Abdullah's white robes swung wildly around him as he left the stables and went to his Silver Cloud Rolls. Back straight, chin pointing upward under his long, black, bearded face, he snatched the cell phone from his bodyguard, who was holding the open car door for him. The other guards maneuvered into position—surrounding the sheik. They filed into their respective vehicles, waiting for him to give the signal.

In a loud, irritated voice, he said into his cell phone before climbing into the vehicle, "Find the broker, Jack Lafferty, Saheed." His face twisted into a deep purple and red color, and his voice carried to all who surrounded him.

"Take care of it today. I paid three million for that horse. I will not be made a fool. Make sure he understands what it is to try to cheat the sheik. Do you understand? Yes, and then… remove Kamal from my sight." He hung up, nodding to his bodyguard who snapped the door shut.

Within minutes, they roared out of the farmyard, gravel spraying under the tires. The Rolls fishtailed down the long, winding road between white fences alongside the green pastures. Hundreds of thoroughbred racehorses grazed in the lush green fields.

THIRTY-SIX
BLACKROCK ISLAND

Returning to the island after an afternoon with Murray at the hospital, Miles flew directly into the sun. Pink and red sunrays bathed the Bell Jet Ranger's shell in bright light and reflected its shadow over the Atlantic. The sun slipped into the horizon as they approached the island.

Patricia heard the hum of the helicopter engine and hurried to meet them at the tarmac.

"Tell me about Murray. Will the lad be alright?" she said as they climbed out of the helicopter.

The grim look on Miles' face answered her. "Yes, but he will need time to mend. Broke both legs and an arm. If it wasn't for Laine's quick response, he may have died."

Patricia crossed herself.

Laine walked ahead of the group down the path to the cottage, looking to escape questions for the time being.

The burnt orange sunrays faded as they entered the cottage. The table was set for dinner—bottles of vintage wine were placed in ice buckets on the side cupboard, Waterford stemmed flutes to the right. A glass on the counter was half full of red wine.

"Poor lad. I was worryin' from the time you left," Patricia said, taking a sip. "I've got stew a warmin'. Havin' a wee nip before we start. The soda bread's a finishin'." She opened the refrigerator door and piled food on the table.

"Don't trouble yourself, Patricia." Miles draped his brown leather jacket over the back of the chair, sitting down. "It smells delicious."

"Let me help you," said Laine.

"Freshin' up all. I can manage this." Patricia removed a platter of fruit from the refrigerator and placed it on the table. Crackers came next, then fresh butter. "Go on with you."

"I think I will," Laine said, leaving them. She needed to contact Max again. She thought, I may have compromised my position by attending to Murray. It was necessary—she'd do it again if she had to—if it meant saving his life, but she should have told Max. A memory tugged at her. She would give it more time—try to piece it together.

She dialed Max, but it went to voicemail. "Yellowbird reporting in again," she said and hung up. Plugging in her cell, it began charging on the nightstand next to her bed while she washed up in the bathroom. She did not hear the lighthouse door creak or the footsteps coming down the hall toward her room.

THIRTY-SEVEN

Eamon entered the back door of the kitchen moments after Laine left the room to wash up. It banged shut. Patricia was stirring liquid in a pot on the stove.

"Whiskey, Eamon?" said Miles, sitting at the table.

"Two fingers," Eamon took a chair at the table.

"Jameson okay?" He poured some in a short glass—no ice on his nod. Miles noted the sweat on Eamon's shirt and the white dust. His own shirt had the same dust from the construction site.

"Aye, make it a double." Eamon slid it back across the table to him.

"Sounds good to me." Miles added more whiskey.

They both clinked and downed it in one gulp. It burned as he swallowed. It made him feel good.

"A wee bit thirsty, we are," said Eamon holding up the bottle, questioning Miles if he wanted a refill.

Miles nodded. "I needed that. This was no accident today. Murray is not lax on the job. I wonder what the hell's going on?" He bit into a sliced red apple wedge.

Eamon shrugged, downed his drink, and filled his glass again, adding extra. "Findin' out will be our business, Miles." He jammed a cracker in his mouth and chewed.

"I've been waitin' for the tellin'," said Patricia, adding chunks of potatoes, carrot wedges, cut garlic, sliced onions, and herbs to the copper pot on the gas stovetop. A good measure of Guinness beer was next, smothering the vegetables. The room filled with its sweet smell as she stirred the pot.

"What happened today after you left here?" said Patricia.

Miles said, "We landed in Donegal. Ambulance took us directly to the hospital, and they operated immediately—took five hours. Doctor told us Murray might have punctured a hole in his lungs by the look of the wound in his side. He didn't, so we waited—they set all his bones and gave him morphine. Murray's tough, but this was bad. Bad enough to kill him, but he survived."

"Poor lad." She opened the refrigerator and removed a block of fresh Irish Cheddar and sliced it on a plate. "Does he have family we should be notifyin' of his accident?" She sat adjacent to him at the table, sipping wine, nibbling.

Eamon answered, "Got some family in Limerick." Eamon reached for another cracker. A thick wedge of cheddar was placed on top. Throwing back the rest of his drink, he said, "Shame, if he can't work again. Sticks in me craw." He rose and went to the bottle. "Miles?" He held it up.

Miles nodded. "I've got the lads working on it. Tom and Wilfred are like bloodhounds. If there is something to find, they'll find it."

"Aye," Patricia said getting up, then lining the stew bowls on the counter next to the stove.

Laine entered the kitchen, poured herself a glass of Pommard burgandy, and sat next to Miles. "What a day."

"How are ye farin', Laine?" said Patricia. "Been a day to remember, it has." She ladled the mixture in each bowl, and placed it in front of them.

"This smells wonderful," said Laine.

"Best cook I know," said Eamon. "Been spoilin' me, me whole life, she has. That's the lass, I've loved for some fifty years." He said in a strong lilted voice, slurring his words. "I'll be showin' her how much—after I've had me dinner." He winked at Patricia. Her cheeks turned red as she slid into a chair next to him at the table.

"Eamon Fitzsimon, whiskey has gone to your head. That'll be enough of you this evenin'," she said and patted his hand.

"Aye, luv, you have made me heart warm," he kissed her on the cheek, squeezed her hand in his. Eamon and Patricia exchanged glances, eating their stew.

Miles said to Laine, "There you have it. I never tire of seeing the love they have for each other." Miles watched Laine watching them, smiling. "Been like that since I was a boy."

"There's not a lot of it these days." She looked at her plate.

"You have to know where to find it," Miles said.

"I see," she said, not trusting what he said.

Eamon said, "Hope Murray recovers."

"Do you remember what he said when he was trapped under the scaffolding?" asked Miles.

"Yes, I remember. He repeated names," said Laine. She sipped her wine, taking a bite of stew. "Hmmm, this is delicious, Patricia." She worried he would ask her about her helping Murray, managing the tourniquet. "On the flight, Murray kept repeating the same thing. 'Tell Miles, Donegal's Pub, Rex, and beware of Jack.' I'm not sure what he was talking about."

Eamon said, "Murray said it like it was important for you to know. He was repeatin' it over and over. Couldn't say wot was wot—the pain was in him."

Laine nodded.

"'Laine has troubles a comin' he was saying."

"That's right."

"I don't recognize the names or the connection," said Miles. "Eamon, will you take Murray's place—temporarily—until he comes back? I think he'd like that."

"I'll be havin' the honor," Eamon said.

"Done," said Miles.

They sat in silence for several moments. Eamon moved to help Patricia with the cleaning up. The couple talked quietly amongst themselves at the kitchen sink.

"What is it, Laine?" asked Miles.

"I don't believe in coincidences." She sipped her wine.

"I don't believe in coincidences, either," said Miles in a strong voice.

"Another accident. I am not so sure."

"Something none of us could have foreseen or avoided," said Miles. "Murray was conscience when we left. It'll take him time to heal and to come to terms with it."

"I know," Laine said to Miles in a soft voice. "It's a horrible way to live—not to be in control of our lives, especially our health."

"People can change," Miles said, sipping the last of his whiskey. "Make life better."

"Is it possible?"

"It is."

"I'm not sure—takes time and energy. I did it." She was hoping to draw him out—the whiskey making him talkative.

"What changed for you?"

"I changed myself," she said. She was getting too close, too personal. Miles could compromise her operation. Staying distant and focused was her main objective. Her voice turned hard, professional. "In the States, I run my own business and my father's architectural firm with the help of key associates. I can't afford to get soft."

"What do you mean?"

"I have to stay on top of things. There's a lot to learn since my parents died," she said bitterly, catching her tone, softening it. "For starters, I didn't even know about the land—here—in Ireland."

"There is enough for all of us to learn. One step at a time," he said in a gentle voice.

"Yes, I guess you're right." Laine was please to hear him speak so plainly. "I thought coming to Blackrock to work for you would give me peace of mind. I could start again. Begin again," she said, despite the caution inside her.

"I'll be here, if you need to talk. We all have our secrets."

"I don't know why, but I believe you." Inside herself she was not smiling at all. Max warned her about getting too close to the subject. It was clear to her to stop, step back from her feelings. "I think I'll have a shot of that whiskey, if you don't mind."

"I'll get it." He went to the cupboard.

The shutters slapped rhythmically against the outside walls of the cottage.

"The shutters be bangin' my head in—thought you'd fixed 'em, luv," said Patricia, covering her ears. "The wind's a tearin' 'em loose from the hinges—another storm's a comin'."

"Aye," he said, downing the rest of his drink. "Be fixin' it—after the whiskey cake, luv."

"Can't you be doin' it now, while we're waitin' for the cake to cool, while I'm doin' the icin'?"

"Aye." Eamon frowned. The door slammed shut when he left.

THIRTY-EIGHT

Outside the cottage, the light from the kitchen burned brightly against the darkness. Slap, slap, slap, the wind blew the wood against the cottage. Shutters groaned under the weight, hanging on a single hinge, lopsided, banging against the cottage wall. Eamon shined the flashlight on hinges worked loose from the foundation. It would only take a minute or two to adjust them. Odd, he thought, he had fixed them a few days ago. The breeze felt good to him—he liked the outdoors.

He went into the mudroom for tools. Carrying the handled metal box, he stopped outside and studied the sky above the Atlantic. He knew storm petrels snuggled into their nests for the evening in the cliffs. The birds were silent, no more exchange of tweets or squawks. Dark clouds sailed past a full moon. He was at peace as he watched the wind bend the tops of the tall trees. It was nearing complete darkness, except for the light of the moon.

Living on the island gave him a sense of how life worked. He knew things—nature's force and the danger it presented. It made him feel alive.

Eamon pictured himself as a child with his father. He remembered stories his father told him of the bears, wolves, owls, and snakes infusing the darkness on missions of search and destroy on the island. He told him they needed to hunt and prey on the smallest of creatures—taking their lives before theirs were taken. They slithered and crept boldly from their hiding places in the night. It was their means of survival. His father told him to observe them—learn from them—use his instincts. He took his advice. Spent his life loving the island. Learning from it—like his father before him.

The silence, except for the wind, filled him with pride. He felt good. Patricia would be wanting to serve the cake. Enough daydreaming.

Curious, he thought, as he pointed his light at the empty holes in the hinges. The screws were not there. He shined his beam on the ground spotting several in the dirt. He felt someone watching him. His instincts kicked in, but not in time. Something hard struck him in the back of the head, knocking him to the ground.

Dazed, he sprang up and shouted, "Bugger!" In boxing stance, he lashed out, balled fists, swinging wildly in the air. Coming full circle, he connected with a punch. He popped his fists in front of himself again, missing—hitting air. He couldn't make out the man in black who hit him. Covering his eye, the man swore. He ran toward the cliff and disappeared down the steps.

"I'll kill you if I catch you around here again," he shouted after him, struggling to keep his balance. Feeling nauseous, his vision clouded, knees buckled, and he pitched forward to the ground. He vomited. As he crawled into the mudroom, the room swam around him, dipping and weaving in and out of his vision as he tried to focus. Hoisting himself up, he swayed back and forth, taking small steps toward the kitchen. "Dirty bugger," he slurred. "Me head." The room went black, and he collapsed on the floor.

What seemed like hours, but in fact was several minutes later, he blinked his eyes open, trying to get his bearings. He was face down on a mop, but where? He recognized the mudroom. His mind was foggy as he lifted himself up. His head ached. He managed to stand and stumbled through the door into the kitchen—into the light— the brightness hurt his eyes. His legs wobbled as he fought to keep himself upright. He leaned against the door jam, breathing heavily.

Miles and Laine were deep in conversation, now staring at him.

"Miles, lad, I'm seeing two of ye'," he said in a low, rough voice. "Me head is cracked." As he gripped the doorknob, his legs slipped out from under him. Pitching face first onto the kitchen floor, he groaned as the wood met his cheek.

Patricia, cutting the cake, saw what happened and ran to his side. "Eamon, Eamon, there's blood running down your shirt," Patricia said. "Back of your head is coshed."

"Shutter tore loose—hit me from behind."

"Hang in there," said Miles, helping him into a nearby chair.

Patricia pulled ice from the refrigerator, wrapped it in a towel, and pressed it on the wound to stop the bleeding. She said in a concerned voice, "Don't be worried."

Laine watched from her chair, resisting the urge to help. Not wanting to draw attention to herself, she stayed seated. Quiet. Listening.

"I was going about fixin' the shutters when someone clobberd me in me noggin'—close to dyin' I am," he said in a weak voice. I'll be needin' a whiskey to help me heal me head." He smiled at Patricia.

"We'll see," she said, holding the ice to his head. Patricia did not smile.

"I socked the bugger, I did—got 'em good, after he hit me. He'll be having a black eye, he will. But me poor head. Don't go after 'em, Miles.

Went off into the woods he did—long gone by now."

"Who?" Miles said.

"The bloke who hit me. Haven't you been listening?"

"Did you recognize him?" said Miles.

"No. We'll be lockin' the doors tonight."

"Eamon, you need a doctor," said Patricia.

"Tis only a scratch. Me head's hammerin' and a poundin'," he said, rubbing the back of his head. He fisted his hands and tried to stand. He swayed from side to side, gave up, and fell back into the chair. "Ach, me noggin' is achin'."

Miles and Laine exchanged a look of concern.

"Can you describe him?" asked Miles.

"I told you, lad, don't ye hear me?" Lines creased his forehead, eyes wrinkled in the corners. "Hit from behind I was. Don't know who did it, but when I find him, I'll show him what for," he said, and moaned. "Stop your fussin'," he said to Patricia, who was patting his head with a towel. "Another whiskey will fix me—keep me from dyin'."

Patricia smiled at him, saying nothing.

Miles said. "Quite a lump you'll have, Eamon. Take a lot more than a tap on the head to make you stay down."

"Aye," said Eamon. "I'll take that bugger down next time we meet, I will." He clenched his fists again, looked to see if Patricia was watching.

"I'll be right back," Miles said. He went outside into the yard and came back with a large flashlight. "There's blood on this, Eamon. Your blood." Miles examined the flashlight. "Heavy duty construction-type flashlight. Might have been outside watching us. But why, is what I want to know."

"Aye, me too," he said. "Hit me with it, he did. You think I made it up?" He tried to get up again, but slumped back in the chair. "I was tellin' you true."

"Like you said, they're gone," said Miles. He walked over to the kitchen door, locking it. "I believe you," Miles said. "Can you describe the man?"

"I didn't see a thing. Knocked me down. Took off—after I hit 'em," said Eamon, smiling. "All dressed in black with a hood over his head."

Miles said, "Okay, we'll get to the bottom of it. Let's get some rest and we'll talk about this in the morning."

"Hope you're alright," said Laine. Another report for Max—the violence was escalating. Someone was making their lives miserable—but who? Everyone in the room was a target. If they wanted Eamon dead, he would have been. It was a warning.

"I'll notify Tom and Wilfrid. I want you to know we'll find out who did this, Eamon."

"I live here. This is my home. We'll have none of it again," Eamon said.

Miles said, "I'll install alarms and sensors tomorrow. That'll put a stop to this."

There it was, Laine thought. A lot of trouble to go through for someone who wants to hurt Miles and his friends. Miles was no pushover.

THIRTY-NINE
DONEGAL HARBOR

The next day, they decided to leave the island and do some shopping in town for the lighthouse. They were in Donahue's Pub at eleven o'clock in the morning ordering brunch, watching the boats coming and going in and out of the harbor. The sun bounced off the ripples in the water surrounding the boats.

Laine said to Miles while they were sipping coffee, "I can't believe it." Putting her hand up to stop him from talking, she said in an excited voice. "The blonde woman. I saw that woman with John in the square the day I landed. She's on that cruise ship down there."

"Are you sure?"

Laine gave him a frantic look, threw her napkin on the table, and grabbed her bag.

"I'm going to talk to her. See what she knows about John."

"I'll go with you." He left money for the bill on the table and followed her out the door.

They made their way down along the wharf to the pier and climbed the metal gangway to the waterbus. They were prevented from entering the boat by a chain link on the railing. Miles hailed the captain who stood on the aft deck consulting a crewman.

"Excuse me, permission to come aboard?" Miles said.

"We've already boarded, sir. Ship is full for this tour. You'll have to wait for the 3:00 p.m. cruise."

The captain watched them.

"No, we're not going on the cruise," said Miles. "I just need to speak to the captain for a minute."

"You have a woman in your crew?" said Laine, frowning, in a loud voice.

"You mean Marla?" said the crewman walking over to them at the rail.

"If you say so," said Laine. "I need to talk to her."

"Marla O'Brian?" said Miles.

"Aye, the only woman aboard *Morrigan*—Marla narrates the cruises. May I ask what ye want her for, sir?"

"The Captain came to them and said in a loud voice, "I'll take it from here. Can I help you?"

"I need to talk to Marla for a few minutes, if that's possible," said Laine in a light voice, smiling her biggest smile at him. "May we please come aboard? It's very important that I speak with her."

The Captain said, "Aye, if it's that important, but you only have a few minutes. We're on a schedule."

The crewman unhooked the chain and extended a hand to Laine onto the ship. "Watch your step."

"Where can I find her?" Laine asked him.

"Last time I saw her she was in the wheelhouse," said the captain. "Take her there now. We have to leave before the tide goes out, so you have to make it short."

"I won't be long," said Laine, following the crewman.

Miles said, "I'll wait here." Then to the captain, "Been wanting to take the tour, but never made time."

"Should take the trip. It tells the history of the area and talks about the famine that took place," Captain said.

"I'm Miles Bourke," he said, extending his hand for a shake. "Don't think we've ever met."

"I've heard of you—you've got the racehorses in Blacksod. Beauties, from what I hear," the captain said. "We can talk while I check my course."

Miles said, "I'd like that. Fine waterbus. Looks brand new."

"It is. We upgraded a few years ago." He and the captain went into the navigation room to talk.

"Up them steps there," the crewman said, leading Laine. "Marla will be checkin' her microphone—settin' up for the cruise. I have to get to my station. I'll be leavin' you here."

Laine entered the wheelhouse. The blonde woman was plugging a microphone into the console, flipping switches. "Testing," she said into the handheld speaker, holding in the button. "Testing—one, two, three."

"Hello," said Laine. "Can I talk to you for a minute?"

Marla whirled around, microphone in hand. She took a sharp breath at the sight of Laine. "No, I'm busy. How'd you get up here anyway? It's only for the captain and crew."

"Captain told me to bring her up," said the crewman, leaving them alone.

Laine studied Marla's fingers clicking the microphone button on and off, ignoring her. She behaved badly.

"Are you Marla?"

"Who wants to know?"

"I do," Laine said in a strong voice, stepping in toward her, closing the distance between them. "I'm Laine Sullivan, John's wife."

"Who's John?" Marla asked, slamming the microphone down on the console, putting her back to Laine and flipping through a manual.

"Don't play innocent with me," Laine said in an angry tone. "I saw you with him in *Donegal Town Square*. He's my husband. His name is John Rafferty and you were there with him." Laine felt the anger inside her. The woman was lying. She would pry the information out of her.

"I don't know no 'John Rafferty.' I've got work to do. So if you don't mind, you need to leave."

"I'll repeat myself. Miles and I saw you Sunday in Donegal Town Square. The two of you were arguing in front of St. Patrick's Church. I know what I saw."

"I don't know what you're talking about." Marla tossed the manual aside and her fingers drummed on the ship's wheel. "I haven't been to church since… hell, I don't know how long. I'm too busy with the cruises." She picked up her microphone again and pushing in the button said, "One, two, three, testing. Embarkation point of emigrants to Canada and North America during famine years is up ahead on the starboard side of the ship. Departure point of coffin ships on your right." Click, click, click sounded the microphone switch.

Laine saw the red nails and lips, long blonde hair—definitely the woman with John. She was smiling.

"What were you doing with my husband?"

"You're nuts, lady. Stop wasting my time—I'm working here—are you deaf?" Marla pressed a button and the ship's horn blared long and sharp drowning out Laine when she tried to speak. She pressed the button a second time, holding the button in longer, the blast piercing their ears.

"Tell me where he is," Laine shouted above the horn's wailing. "I need to talk to him."

"You bitch. I've got work to do." Marla held down a third long blast. "Get out of my wheelhouse. I don't have time for this." She shoved Laine aside and went below, taking the stairs to the door marked *Private Crew's Quarters*. She slammed it in Laine's face.

Laine's eyes narrowed into thin lines when she heard the lock. "I'm going to find out what you're hiding," she said in a loud voice. "Believe it." Laine thought, I'll have Max run her name—get whatever he can. "You have not seen the last of me." Laine shouted at the closed door. "You're lying, Marla. One way or another I'll find him. Bet on it." She raised her voice. "I'll be seeing you again—real soon."

Laine walked to the stern of the boat to meet Miles. He was talking to the captain.

"Let's go," she said in a hard voice.

"Sure," he said. To the captain he said in a strong voice, "Thanks for the information. I'll follow up on it."

They walked down the metal gangway to the dock.

"You okay? You look angry."

Laine's face was tight and her grip hard on his arm hard. She said nothing. They stopped at the end of the pier and she looked back at the ship. Marla was standing with the captain, rubbing his back, kissing him.

"Miles, look at her. She's got her hands all over the captain. Last week my husband—now him—she's something else." Laine said in an irritated voice, "She behaved badly in the wheelhouse. She wouldn't tell me anything. Kept pressing the damn horn."

Miles stared at Marla. "She was wild when we were growing up—had a mean streak. Drowned her cat and bragged about it to anyone who would listen. Thought it was funny."

"You know her?" her voice was high.

There was a silence.

"Yes, much to my regret. There was another thing… her father drowned off Donegal Bay. They say the boat had a hole smashed in it, right under the gas can. Someone put tape on it to cover it up. Police thought it was Marla, but they couldn't prove it. She was only twelve and she lived with her mother at her grandparent's home. Her father left them. She hated it and him. Stay away from her. She's bad."

"I am, but I wanted information. She lied about being in the square with John."

"Wish I could help," said Miles.

"Thanks, you've got enough on your plate," she said. "It is all very strange." She thought, Max could pull up the police report on Marla and she would know whom she was dealing with. It was worse than she thought. "Let's head back to the island."

"Sure," he said. "Guess you didn't find out what you were hoping for."

"It's frustrating, Miles. I told you. She blasted the damn horn every time I tried to talk to her." Laine turned on her heel and stormed away from him. "I'm at a dead end."

"I've got an idea," Miles said in a strong voice. "Let's go to Margaret Hogan's real estate office while we are in town, find out if she knows anything about Marla and the man she was with. She knows all the town gossip."

Her voice softened and she said, "Good idea. Well then… let's have lunch first, since I ruined breakfast."

"I was hoping you'd say that."

Laine and Miles walked into Donahue's Pub, and he asked for a table by the window facing the harbor.

The sun was high noon over Donegal Bay by the time the *Morrigan* cruised out of the harbor. People waved from their seats, taking pictures. Powerboats, curraghs, and sailboats glided into the bright blue-green waves of the Atlantic Ocean, beyond the bay.

After the wait staff had served their drinks, spinach salad, and grilled salmon, Laine observed the activity on the pier.

"I don't believe what I'm seeing," she said setting down her ice tea. "Marla is not on the ship. She and *John* just drove out of the pier parking lot in a Ford, dark blue pick-up truck. I knew it."

FORTY

BLACKROCK ISLAND

It was after midnight when Marla and Jack hid the curragh around the corner from the cove on Blackrock Island for the third time in the last few days. Jack had pushed up his plans after he had forgotten the sheik's horse at the auction.

Jack said, "Wait here."

Marla said, "Whatever you say, Jack. Let's get this over with. I can't keep doing this with you. We need money to disappear for a while—and get Kamal off your back. Jerk almost killed you when he found out you swindled the sheik. He'll come after you again."

Jack stared at her smiling.

"Be sure of it. Those people do not play around. Sure you can handle it?" She stretched her legs in the boat and leaned back in the seat, pulling the zipper of her black jacket up to her neck.

"Haven't I been handling it?" Jack's eyes narrowed at her. "I am handling it."

"Yeah, sure you are," she said in a low tone. "Get going. I'm already sick of waiting."

"I'll be back in no time, and this time with Laine," he said and smiled at her.

"I am waiting and ready to be done with this. If you aren't here in an hour, we go to Plan C."

"Yeah, yeah, yeah, there's no plan C. We'll be done with this tonight. You'll see," he laughed at his bad joke and Marla gave him a sour look.

Leaving from the beach, he quickly took the path through the forest toward the lighthouse. He memorized it the night he hit Eamon on the head. Making good time, he scrambled down the cliff and up the stone stairs to the tunnel. Taking out his small penlight, he ran in the wet, dark tunnels to the place where Marla had shown him the fireplace hatch. Reaching the opening, without getting lost, was a first for him—and not hitting his head on the damn rock.

"I know these tunnels as good as Marla," he said in a hard voice. "Have to tell her—rub it in. She's getting on my nerves."

He stretched out uncomfortably on the jagged rock floor above the hatch and listened, pressing his ear to the crack. He heard breaking glass and loud voices coming from the room below.

He heard Laine say, "Oh Miles, I'm sorry."

"Oh Miles, I'm sorry," he mocked her to himself. She would be sorry—soon—very soon.

"Don't worry about it, Laine," said a man's loud voice. "It's only a glass. I have more. Don't do that. I'll clean it up."

"It's no bother," Jack heard Laine say in a light voice.

Miserable bitch, he thought. She's caused me a lot of trouble. You're gonna have more to worry about than spilling your fancy glass, honey.

The cold floor was giving him a headache. Sitting up he lit a cigarette, inhaling in the dark. *How long am I going to have to wait here? This is ridiculous.* He was getting cold and thirsty.

Jack heard a different voice through the crack. He bent awkwardly to listen. The woman's voice had a heavy Irish lilt to it. *Loud mouth and bossy,* he thought.

"Here's a another plate of starters for the both of ye. Eamon, me luv, set them on the table just there." He heard the scrape of chairs. "We'll be sittin' down to a lovely meal, we will."

What does she mean—starters—sitting down? Jack dropped his cigarette on his leg, burning a hole in his jeans.

"Shee—ite …" he stifled a shout as the butt burned his skin. He knocked it off his leg.

It flew in the air, hissing as it landed on watery ground. His leg burned as he pulled the scorched material away from the singed flesh. "Owe, that hurts. Hell with it." He put his head back on the hatch crack, listening.

A man's voice, probably the one the bossy woman called Eamon, answered, "Aye. Here you are. Bringin' you me favorite—crab cakes. Made by me own wife, they are. Fresh caught from the sea, they was, and cooked up lovely."

Jack heard the sound of plates clattering. *They are eating down there on top of that pile of junk. I'm gonna be here all night at this rate.* Something crawled across his face, and he smacked it with his hand. "Damn thing bit me," he said in a low painful voice. He shut his mouth realizing his mistake—they might have heard him. He waited—they were still talking. A welt rose on his cheek. It was itchy; he scratched it until it bled, swiped it with his hand, and rubbed it on his pants. Sitting on the hard floor, legs numbing, he lit another cigarette. Inhaling, he waited.

"Patricia makes 'em the best there is," said the man's loud voice.

Then Laine's voice said, "Better tack that tarp back on the window,

Miles, the rain's coming in."

Jack said in a low voice under his breath, "Did she say rain? Marla's goin' to be a raving lunatic if she gets soaked. Damn it."

"Heard a nor'easter is forecasted. There'll be another storm tonight."

Jack heard hammering.

"That does it," said Miles. "The tarp will hold for now." The loud mouth woman's Irish voice said, "I think we'd better eat in the cottage. It's getting dark and cold in here."

"You're the cook," said Miles. "Let's pack everything and head in."

"Aye, a terrible storm's a brewin'," said the other man's voice. "Come up from the cove half hour ago. Lines on the boats tore loose—fixed 'em good as new. They were a bouncin' around like corkscrews."

Jack pressed his ear closer to the hatch. The man's speech was harder to understand.

Miles said, "Right, it's best if we go down again before we eat. Take another look."

"One broke free of its moorings—but I got it cleated. You don't want to go down those stone steps in this storm, lad. There're slippery-like when it rains."

Patricia said, "There's only the platter and glasses. Eamon can carry 'em. Come on now. We'll eat and then you'll go."

"I'll be down in a minute," said Laine. "I'll grab my designs and finish up in the house tonight. There's not enough light in here to see anything."

"Odd thing," Jack heard Eamon say. "When I was doin' the fastenin' up at the cove, me eyes sighted a small curragh pulled up on the beach. It was past the point—hidin' it was. No one lookin' after it."

Great, thought Jack. Just great. They saw the boat. Where the hell was Marla?

Miles answered, "I'll get my rain jacket. Eamon, get yours. Let's check it out."

"Aye," said the other man.

Jack scrambled to his feet. *Damn it. Marla. Why didn't you cover the boat with something?* He stood there, thinking. *How the hell can I grab Laine, if they leave the tower and go down to the boat?*

He heard Miles say, "See if someone is on the island—another stranger won't be leaving without us knowing why he is here. You can be sure of it."

"I'll keep the supper heated on low in the cottage," said the woman with the lilt in her voice. "Take your time. Laine, do you need help?"

"No, thanks, Patricia. I can manage."

Jack heard the Patricia woman say, "I'll see you downstairs then." Her voice faded.

Jack heard footsteps fading away. He waited a moment. He pressed his ear tightly against the hatch. Nothing. As quietly as he could he pulled open the hatch, careful not to drop it on his lap. She had to be alone getting her things.

Gradually, step-by-step, he lowered himself into the fireplace and peered into the room. *Yes, she was there with her back to him.* Everyone else had gone. Good, he thought.

She was humming to herself while she was putting papers in her briefcase.He pulled the cloth from his pocket and quickly poured the chloroform on it. Treading silently, swiftly to her, he wrapped his arms around her neck from behind. Pressing the cloth over her nose and mouth, he held tight. She struggled and jabbed him with her elbows, but he dodged the move. She twisted and kicked backward connecting with his shin, but his boot took the blow. She was good, but not good enough, he thought.

After a short time, he felt her go limp. She was heavy in his arms, legs bending at the knees—a dead weight. Pressing the cloth tighter against her face, she slumped against him—unconscious. He waited a few more seconds and removed the cloth. He could hear her shallow breathing. He had to hurry, before she came to. He admired her beauty—what a knockout.

"Such a shame," he said in a hard voice. "But I need your money, honey." He laughed.

Laine groaned. "Sheiks don't like to be cheated. Kamal's going to kill Marla and me if I don't get your money and get the hell out of town. So you see, darling, that's where you come in. It was always about the money, honey," he said, laughing. "I need that money." He soaked the cloth with more chloroform and pressed it to her face—just in case. He waited. "That'll last for a few more minutes, anyway. It'll be nice to take a trip to Costa Rica. I've never been there. Marla hasn't either. You're gonna make that happen for us." He said in an arrogant tone, "Time to go, babe."

Jack grunted as he hefted her over his shoulder and scaled the notches inside the fireplace. At the top, he stuffed her through the hatch. She was light, and it made it easy for him to maneuver her through the opening.

Once inside the tunnel, he dragged her to the side wall. Slamming the hatch shut, he took a deep breath and hoisted her over his shoulder. He fumbled inside his jacket pocket for his penlight. Finding it, he jammed it into his mouth, and the small beam led the way down the winding tunnel.

After a short time, he forked right. Now, he heard the roar of the ocean and the howling wind outside the tunnel. It was getting colder and the dampness clung to his skin. Laine was getting heavier with every step. He tripped and dropped her.

"Damn it Laine. Lose some weight, you bitch," he said in an angry tone. He dragged her up over his shoulder and repositioned her on the other side. Her shoe fell off, but he ignored it. He was in a hurry.

The cave room was around the next bend. He made it without further mishap. At the entrance, he managed to squeeze Laine through the narrow rock opening. Her head bounced off the stone slab when he dropped her on the bed-like rock ledge against the wall.

"Oops," he said, and laughed. "Gonna have a little headache, honey, but you'll never feel it. We're in a hurry, so you stay here for a minute. I'll be right back."

Placing his finger under her nose, he felt her irregular breathing.

"Maybe another dose." He fished the cloth from his pocket.

At that moment, Laine's eyes opened. She coughed. Coughed again. She tried to rise from the ledge, but Jack's arms held her down. She struggled against his hold. Her eyes grew wide. "John! It's me, Laine—your wife. What are you doing? Are you crazy?"

She saw the cloth near her face and turned her head away toward the wall, struggling to move away from it. She raised her knees and punched at him with both fists, but missed. He grabbed her wrists. She was weak, and he held both of them in one hand. Without a word, John clamped the cloth over Laine's mouth and nose while she called out his name.

She thrashed about with all her strength and tried to yank free of his hands, but he was too strong for her. She stopped struggling and her body went limp, eyes closed, knees flat on the slab. John removed the cloth.

"Too bad that scaffolding didn't take care of you instead of Murray. Now you are going for a long swim in the ocean—call it your last boat ride, honey." He said in a hard voice, "That oughta' keep you for a while. At least till I get back." He whispered in her ear, "Think of it as a late birthday present. This time, I won't be disappearing—you will." He covered her with the tarpaulin he had left there earlier and slipped out of the cave.

FORTY-ONE

In the tunnel, Jack lit a cigarette and threw the match on the ground. The path led him outside and he climbed to the top of the cliff to look for Miles and the other man. He did not see them.

"Well, guess I'll have to meet Marla and we'll go for plan C. She is going to be really mad," he said in an anxious voice. "Too bad. She'll be happy when we get out of here."

Laine laid there, looked through her partially open eyes—she was alone. In her covert ops training, she had been taught to hold her breath, when attacked with chemicals—like the one John gave her. She did, but the drug got in her system from the extra dose. She had underestimated him. Keep moving, she told herself. You've got to get out of here, before he gets back. Sitting up, the room spun around her. She gulped in the damp air to clear her head and swung her legs over the side of the rock slab. It only took her a second to kick off her single shoe, grab the penlight he had dropped on the floor, and run blindly into the tunnel.

She heard the ocean. The sound directed her to it. She saw the stone ledge at the end of the tunnel. She ran to it and stepped outside. The surrounding area was deserted. She flew down the stone stairs to the cove where Miles' boat was docked. Quickly, she sped up the next set of stone steps to the top of the cliff.

The going was slippery as the wind and rain pelted her—refreshed her. She welcomed it, but the stones tore at her bare feet. At the top, she ran across the yard and shoved her way into the cottage kitchen.

Patricia dropped the platter she was setting on the table, seeing Laine soaked and filthy. "For the luv of Mary," she said, crossing herself. "Look like you've seen a ghost."

Laine locked the door behind her and said in a hard voice, "I did. Don't let anyone in. I'm getting my gun." She ran out of the kitchen and down the hall. "I'll be right back," she said in a loud voice over her shoulder.

Patricia crossed herself again. "Her gun. It's a dark day, it is." She locked the door.

Grabbing a sharp knife from the counter, she put it in the pocket of her apron and snatched the phone from the table. Pressing it tightly to her ear, she dialed the police.

"Tom, ye gotta come to the island quick. Somethin's a foot. Laine came in all beat up. Goin' for her gun." She nodded the reply. "We'll be waitin' for you. Miles and Eamon are out on the property. Eamon found an empty curragh beached 'round the end of the point. They're carryin' the rifles, they are—huntin' them in the dark," she said in a strong voice. "Combin' the island in the storm—left half hour ago. Strangers hid the boat, they did— but Eamon saw it and told Miles. Come quick. We need you here."

The rain pelted the cottage as she looked out the window.

She patted her pocket. "Aye, I'll use me knife if I have to," she said. "Don't have a good feelin' bout this." She listened. "Half hour, you say?" She waited. "By boat." She relaxed her grip on the phone. "Bring all yer boys, Tom—got a bad feelin' 'bout this. There's trouble a brewin' on Blackrock. Aye, that it is."

She hung up, sat in a chair at the table, watching the door—waiting for Laine to return—with her gun.

FORTY-TWO
KOOLMOORE STABLES

On the mainland inside Koolmoore Stables, Kamal, on his knees, cowered before Sheik Abdullah. "Forgive me, my brother."

"Forgive you? Your face offends me. A woman bested you? You let that broker Jack swindle us. You let them get away." The sheik's eyes narrowed. "Tell me."

"She tore my face with her red nails—tied her to a chair in the hotel—but…." he said, and bowed lower to the sheik.

"Hotel. You were in a hotel with a woman? Infidel." Sheik Abdullah flew into a rage, slapping Kamal in the face over and over again. "You let this happen." The guards watched a few feet away, not moving. They said nothing, stood at attention.

"It's not what you think, my brother," he felt the blood trickle from his mouth. He bowed low and pressed his head to the floor, waiting for the next blow. It came as a kick to his ribs. He fell and righted himself, gasping, bowing over and over at the feet of the sheik. "Forgive me, my brother, I was there to pick up the money. The horse is dead."

"It's been two days since I've heard from you," the sheik said in a loud, hard voice. "Where is my money?" His hand drew back to strike him. "Tell me."

Kamal cringed before the man in the white robes. "The woman escaped. I left her for a moment only. The maid freed her." The corner of his mouth turned up. "But I took care of the maid."

"Silence," roared the sheik. He raised his hand and struck Kamal again. "You told me the woman would lead you to the American broker and my money. She didn't. You failed me. My horse is dead. You have sealed your fate."

Turning to his bodyguards, he nodded. The men moved swiftly and dragged Kamal along the marbled alley toward the black limousine waiting in the yard.

"Please, my brother, I beg you. Give me another chance," Kamal cried. His long white robes swept the smooth marble floor of the stables. He swiveled his head, pleading for forgiveness. His eye was swollen shut.

"Your chances are over. Praise Allah," said the sheik. The bodyguards dragged him out the door. "Get him out of my sight."

The horses whinnied and stomped their hooves in the stalls, heads jerking up and down. "Shut them up," said the sheik in a loud, hard voice to one of the groomsmen. "Where is the headman?"

"There is no headman—now." The boy motioned toward Kamal. He bowed lower and lower.

"Look at me." The sheik glared at him and said, "You are my new headman. Fetch my horse. I'm going riding." He stamped his foot. "Don't make me wait."

"Yes, my brother." The boy bowed over and over, backing away.

The sheik waited in the yard for the Arabian Kamal had purchased from Bourke.

"Here he is, my brother." He grabbed the sleeve of his own robe and polished the seat of the saddle before the sheik could mount. The reins were jerked from his hands as the sheik mounted, took them, and kicked the horse into a gallop.

"You will do well for me," the sheik said as he charged out of the yard. Snapping his whip against the horse's side, he jumped the nearest fence into the pasture.

FORTY-THREE
BLACKROCK ISLAND

The sea smelled of storm. Frigate birds nested in their caves on the side of the cliffs as Jack picked his way above them through the forest, away from the cave and Laine.

"Damn her," he said as he struggled to see where he was going. "I dropped my damn light. When I get back to the cave, I am going to make her pay." Rain slashed his face as he peered below, seeing nothing but darkness. He groped his way through the wet leaves and branches clawing and ripping his shirt, scratching his arms and face. In a short time, he made it to the shore where he and Marla hid the boat.

"Damn," he said, dodging behind a tree. A police patrol boat cruised into the inlet, lights flashing on the shore where he had stood. He thought, just my luck.

Jack crouched low and watched them. A man stood in the bow of the police boat, floodlight pointing to the beach around the end of the point where they landed the curragh. The policeman waved his arms and directed his boat to the spot where they had disembarked. Another group of men were on the beach waving their flashlights. They marched over the stony ground toward the curragh. Jack pulled his black cap low and waited, pressing himself into the ground on the edge of the cliff, watching them. Where was Marla? Good thing he had another plan—ready and in place.

Jack scrambled back into the forest, slipping on the rocky surface. He scraped his right knee, ripped his pant leg, and stepped into a thorny bush, tearing the flesh on his arms.

"Damn," he said, backing out. The rain was icy. He lost his footing and slid down a slight incline, grabbing a branch to break his fall. The wind punished him. He flattened himself against the cliff and shoved his foot into the nearest niche. His hat blew off.

"Damn," he said again, as he trod slowly into the dense forest. "I can't see where I'm going. This is nuts."

He realized he was on the path he had taken earlier in the day, but it became more treacherous in the heavy rain and wind. He flattened his belly on the ground again and lay there catching his breath, looking over the edge. The men were searching the area.

Dozens of sparkler-like lights lit up the night on the beach below him. He was above the boat, but high up on the cliffs to the right of them. Rocks dug deep into his chest and knees. He was soaked. He checked his watch. It had taken him more than a half hour to make the ten-minute return trip to the boat in daylight, but tonight was different. It took longer in the dark with no light to guide him.

He estimated it would take at least another half hour to get the boat in a position to carry Laine out to sea without being seen—if they left. If not, he would initiate Plan B. Marla hated Plan B, but she would have to suck it up, he thought.

Going on, he wound through the dense forest and made his way down to the small inlet.

No one would believe a dead husband would come back to haunt her, let alone kill her, he thought.

Going over to a place he had marked on the beach, he dug under the rocks and uncovered the plastic bag holding the wetsuits and extra life jackets they had brought with them. Marla had buried them when Jack went to get Laine. Her wet suit was still in the bag. Ripping off his wet clothes, he rolled them into a heap and stuffed them into the bag. Shrugging into his wetsuit warmed him. They had a good plan. It was working. He pulled on the hood, gloves, and boots. Perched on the top of his head, he adjusted the facemask. He uncovered the oxygen tank and weight belt. He strapped it on. He was ready.

After he dressed, he climbed up a short incline on the cliff and pulled off the tree branches covering the inflatable boat and engine. He unhooked the line from the tree that held it fast. Wading into the icy water, he pushed the boat in backward and lowered his oxygen tank into the bottom of the boat. Climbing in the boat, he sloshed through the water, sat, and placed the tank by his feet. He crouched over on the wood plank, and bailed the excess water out of the bottom. Next, he ran his hand under the console, locating the key to the small engine. He smiled.

The wind covered the sound of the engine when he turned the key. It sputtered and quit. A wave hit the boat broadside, tipping him backward into the bottom of the boat. He slammed his head against the oxygen tank.

"Sheeit," he said, rubbing his head. He got back up, grabbed an oar, and shoved off the bottom of the ocean, pushing the boat out into the waves and away from the shore.

The boat pitched and rolled in the unforgiving water. It slammed against the waves, leaning heavily on its side, but didn't overturn. He braced himself, jamming the oar into the water again, but it was too deep to touch bottom. The waves were wild. He grabbed the oars and rowed until he was away from the beach. He turned the key again. It caught.

"I did it," he said in a strong voice.

Throwing the throttle in reverse, he managed to maneuver the curragh away from the shallow water. Waves tossed him from side to side, but the boat picked up speed and he sliced through the water. He rode the waves like a surfer, keeping on the top of the waves, so he would not overturn. He took in his surroundings as water filled the bottom of the boat. He headed toward the mainland, leaving the searchlights behind him.

The rain beat down on his facemask and obstructed his view—but he had escaped.

After a while, the wind heightened and gusted around him, making it hard for him to steer. He knew he was at the halfway point when he saw the red buoy. He had timed it perfectly. He was on target—Plan B was working.

He shivered, despite the wetsuit. It was not the cold he was feeling as he rode the dark waves. He went over their plan in his head—tomorrow was not soon enough, he thought.

Jack saw the light on the top of Blacksod Lighthouse in the distance. It was not far. He had made it—he'd make it the rest of the way. He was sure of it.

A bright beam of light from a police boat came directly at him from the east, shattering the darkness. It came as a surprise, and it lit him up like the Fourth of July. Jack left the throttle in full gear. He dropped a life jacket overboard. Donning his weight belt, he grabbed his oxygen tank, and strapped it to his back. He pulled the facemask down over his nose and mouth, securing the strap, and pushed the regulator in his mouth.

Facing backward on the side of the boat, he pulled on his fins. He was ready. He checked the time on his watch, and flipped over the side backward into the water—away from the light. He purged the dive valve in his mouth and descended below the waves.

He dropped down to twenty-five feet, checked his compass, and kicked his fins toward the mainland.

FORTY-FOUR

Laine and Patricia cleaned up the kitchen. Miles and Eamon were combing the property looking for the man who had knocked Eamon on the head. The doors were locked and all the lights in the cottage were on.

All at once, the pantry door flew open and banged heavily against the wall. Laine and Patricia whirled around at the noise.

Laine grabbed the gun from the back of her pants and pointed it in the direction of the noise. She moved to the other side of the kitchen table opposite the pantry door.

"What the hell do you want?" Laine leveled her gun at the blonde woman, cocking the hammer. "You have no business here."

"You really are a dumb bitch," said Marla, ping-ponging her own gun back and forth at the women. "Not so smart now, are you? Think I didn't know where to find you?"

Laine said nothing. She saw the muscles in Marla's face tighten. Red lips formed a tight line. Laine stared at Marla—legs apart—ready to shoot her.

Marla squared her shoulders. "You're coming with me," she said to Laine in a loud, irritated voice. "Yeah, honey, we're going to take a little trip together. Just you and me."

"Hardly. Took you long enough to get here. We've been expecting you for days. You're slow on the uptake." Laine stared at her with hard eyes. "Have a seat," she said, nodding toward a chair. "The men are going to take you on a little jaunt back to the mainland—to jail—where you belong."

"Not in my plans. You're going with me or the old woman gets it."

"Come to kill me, Marla? For John? Guess he botched that for you—too bad." Laine thought, I'll kill her if I have to. Throw her off balance—then react. She steadied her aim, and her fingers tightened on the gun.

"Don't think we can settle this peaceful-like, Marla?" asked Patricia in a soft voice, backing up to the counter, pulling open a drawer. She took something from it and hid it under her apron.

"Shut up, old lady," Marla said, waving her gun at Patricia. "Sit in that chair or I'll kill you."

"I'll shoot you right between the eyes, before you even move a muscle. Count on it." said Laine, giving her a dead stare

Marla was watching Laine, not looking at Patricia. "Shut up, Laine, before I blow her head off. Are you deaf, old woman? I said sit down."

Patricia sat.

Marla said, "Thought you were so smart. Asking me all those questions on the boat. You really are a dumb bitch. I see why John dumped you." She laughed. Eyes narrowing, she said in a high-pitched voice, "We've been planning to kill you ever since we saw you in Donegal. Coming here was a big mistake for you, Mrs. Rafferty."

Laine was feeling bad. In a hard loud voice, she said, "You're the mistake. Leave her out of it," she motioned to Patricia. "I'll go with you. It's not her problem." Laine placed her gun on the table. "There, let's go."

"About time you figured it out. I'm going to shoot her anyway. You're coming with me whether you want to or not." Marla fixed her gun on Patricia. "What the hell?"

"Sit down, girl, or I'll shoot ye dead." Patricia crouched down behind the table and leveled her gun at her. "Old lady, we'll see about that. Drop it or it'll be the last thing you ever do." Patricia fired a shot past Marla's head to the right.

"You're crazy." Marla grabbed a pan from the stove and threw it at her, knocking the gun from her hand. It fell to the floor and went off.

Laine grabbed her gun from the table. "Patricia, get down."

Patricia made herself small under the table, searching for her gun. Finding it she crawled backward into the hallway. At the same time, Marla flipped the lock and dove out the kitchen door leading to the mudroom. Laine dodged behind the wall leading to the hallway. Aiming low and left, she fired at Marla's torso. The bullet tore through the wood door and hit the target.

"Gottcha," said Laine.

"Damn you. Damn you." Marla screamed and fell to her knees. She fired wildly into the room. Sliding backward on the floor, she crouched down. "Bitch. John's bitch." She fired three more times in Laine's direction—missing her.

"Stay where you are," Laine said in a hard, loud, controlled voice. "The next shot will kill you. Give yourself up."

"Screw you." Marla fired another shot hitting the kitchen wall next to Laine's head.

"Missed," Laine said in a loud voice. She dropped to her knees and shot back. The bullet pierced the glass shattering the window of the kitchen door.

The outside door banged shut. Marla said in a angry voice, "It's not over yet. You'll see."

Patricia said in a sad, low voice, "Let her go. The boys will be arrivin'—they can go after her. She's no good."

Laine ignored her. Gun in hand, she slid into the mudroom hugging the wall. Scanning the room, she found it empty. Marla had escaped.

FORTY-FIVE

Now in the kitchen, Laine said, "You can come out Patricia. She's gone."

"For the luv of Mary, who be teachin' you to shoot like that?" Patricia said in a weak voice. She sat at the table and laid her gun on top of it. "You been in trainin', you have."

"It's a long story."

Shouts coming from the front room of the cottage interrupted them. Seconds later, Miles and Eamon ran into the kitchen followed by the policemen Tom and Wilfrid.

"We heard shots," Miles said.

"That you did," said Patricia. "Takin' your time you did with the boys. Laine was keepin' the peace, she was. Should have seen her…"

Laine said, "Marla just left. I shot her."

They stopped and listened.

"She's armed. I saw her head toward the woods." She pointed to the kitchen door.

"We're on it," said Tom. He spoke into his walkie-talkie and updated the peacekeepers who were canvasing the island for John—and now Marla. He directed the troops to set up a perimeter near the woods. "It won't be long—she can't go far. Police boats are looking for Jack, John, whatever he goes by, on the water."

Wilfrid nodded, "We'll get her—and him. Don't be worried. We have officers stationed 'round the house. Protectin' you, they will."

"Then I won't be worryin'," said Patricia.

The men saw the gun on the table and picked it up. Smelled the barrel. "Where did this come from?" Tom asked.

"Aye, that's my gun. Laine's got her own, she does," said Patricia.

Miles eyes widened, looking at Laine. "You have a gun?"

Laine said, "I do, and have a permit for it. Do you need to see it?"

"Don't have time now, lass," said Wilfrid, stepping in. "Plenty of time later. Tom, let's go out back and track Marla down. She can't be far. This one is for the books."

"There's more,' said Laine in a strained voice. "My dead husband kidnapped me a few hours ago here in the map room—on the island. He dragged me through the tunnel, but I escaped when he left me alone for a short time. He said he would be back to take me on a boat. I was in a cave room down by the steps leading to the cove. He may have seen you."

Miles was leaning on the counter. He was studying her, and she felt his eyes on her. He was waiting for her to say something more—explain herself—and the gun.

Patricia said, "Aye, boys go after Marla, be quick about it. She can't be far."

Tom said, "Wilfrid, let's track her down. You take the rear of the house. I'll go round the front."

Wilfrid left.

Tom stopped as he was leaving. Turned to Laine, saying, "Did you say your 'dead husband'?" He looked at Patricia.

Laine spoke up. "Yes, he's alive. He attacked me and drugged me with chloroform. He left me for some reason, but he said he'd be back to kill me. I pretended I was out of it, and I found my way back here." She put her back to the wall, concealing her gun under her shirt.

"Don't worry, lass," said Tom. "We'll catch 'em. Lock all the doors after we leave. Miles and Eamon, search the cave. I know you know how to get there."

Miles opened a drawer and took two flashlights, handing one to Eamon. "I've got extra shells for the rifles. Here's a few more. We'll go through the tunnel." He went to another cupboard, handing them to Eamon. "Lock all the doors and tunnel entrance—don't open any of them." His eyes bore into Laine's—dark and uninviting. They left, slamming the tunnel door behind them.

Laine locked the doors. She wondered what Miles thought of her.

"For the luv of St. Patrick," said Patricia, blessing herself. "Don't you worry, those lads'll find 'em." She went to the living room, Laine following, and they lifted the shotgun from the rack above the fireplace. She handed it to Laine.

"It's loaded. Somethin' tells me ye' know how to use it better than me," she said. "I've got me gun in me pocket. This time, we'll be waitin' for 'em, if they're comin' back."

"Good thinking," said Laine. "I might tell you that story you asked me about—some other day."

"Aye, you will, lass—in time—when you are ready." She pulled out a box of bullets from a bureau drawer. Sliding the lid of the box open, she picked up a few and loaded them into her gun. Patricia spun the barrel in place. "Makin' us safe."

Laine said, "Can you shoot that thing?"

"Aye."

Laine said, "Good."

"I know, lass," she said, walking back into the kitchen. "We'll surprise 'em, won't we?"

"Yes, we will," she said, hesitating, wondering if she should confide in her. "I thought my husband and I had a good life. It was all a lie."

"Some things can't be explained. It's the way people are. Some are bad from the start. Marla's one of 'em, too—maybe that's what she saw in your husband. Hard to be tellin'."

Multiple shots rang out in the yard. An explosion rattled the windows. They saw a burst of fire and it lit the sky around the cottage. Men ran toward the helicopter pad and the woods.

"Oh, no." Laine ran out the door into the back yard, Patricia following. "What happened?" Black smoke filtered to her, making her cough. She covered her nose and mouth with her shirt. Patricia did the same. Fires blazed in front of them, scorching the trees.

A plethora of voices came out of the smoke. Men in black uniforms, gas masks, and rifles marched toward Laine and Patricia, holding out masks.

"Them's the peacekeepers," said Patricia in a rough voice. "Fine troops, they are. Be wantin' a word."

"You there," the man in the lead shouted at them. He handed them masks as more voices materialized—uniformed, armed, boots marching toward them.

Laine watched as Miles' helicopter burned up in front of them.

FORTY-SIX
ATLANTIC OCEAN

Leaving Blackrock, the sea-worthy police patrol boat sliced through the rough ocean searching for the curragh. The white beam of the spotlight swept back and forth across the water, looking for Jack's boat. White caps broke over the top of them, and towering waves rolled them from side to side. They were pitched and heaved about by the movement of the waves, making them uncomfortable. At other times, they were thrown back and forth, bow dipping under the curl of the waves, seeing nothing from the helm but black ocean. Popping out from under the wave, they rode over the next crest, but the boat pounded down in the trough, only to be dipped again. The pounding made it hard for them to talk, jarring their teeth.

"There it is." Captain Robert said in a loud voice to his crew while holding the wheel. "Ahead—off the starboard bow. Thirty degrees." Spray covered the windshield. The flick, flick, flick of the wipers cleared the glass until the next spray.

"Sinking, Captain," said Ogden, peering through binoculars. "Taking its fill of the sea." The darkness of the night enveloped the boat, making it hard to see.

"Don't have much time," said Captain Robert. "Anyone aboard?"

A helmsman directed the white beam of the spotlight on the curragh. "'Tis empty," he said in a sad tone.

"Takin' her in on the starboard side." He said in a loud voice, "Beam the light on it again."

A crewman ran to the stern, slipping on the deck. He grabbed the rail and yelled, "Anyone out there?" The boat rolled from side to side, and salty water washed over the decks. "Life jacket near the engine. Don't see anyone, Captain."

"Affirmative." Captain Robert inched the throttle back, slowing the boat. "See anyone?"

"No," he said in a loud voice. "Fog's comin' in. Makin' it hard to see a thing."

"Over there. Portside, near the stern," a crewman called.

"Hang on," Captain Robert said in a strong voice. "I'll take her port side." As they changed direction, they saw the curragh capsize.

A hugh wave flipped the boat again, dragging the hull under.

The crewman hollered, "It's gone under, Captain. It's no use."

The captain headed ten degrees to port, and the tip of the bow was all that was left of the boat. "We're too late," said Captain Robert in a loud voice. "It's gone under."

"Aye, Aye, Captain," said the man controlling the searchlight.

"Take a few more passes. Check for survivors," he told his crew.

The patrol boat rolled and yawed through the green foam. The wind hummed as they patrolled back and forth, back and forth, finding nothing but dark ocean.

"Wind's picking up," a crewman said to the captain.

"Calling off the search. Make ready for the port," the captain said in a loud voice, gripping the wheel. Crewmen took their positions and prepared the lines to dock.

Blacksod Lighthouse guided them into the harbor where they ended the search. Perished at sea, wrote Captain Robert in the ship's log. He signed it, dated it, and closed the leather-bound volume—ending the search.

FORTY-SEVEN
BLACKROCK ISLAND

At the same time the police were searching the Atlantic, Jack was swimming under the waves toward the mainland. It had been harder than he thought. Exhaustion crept in when he reached the first buoy marking the course for the Olympic Triathlon Swimming Competition.

Taking a moment, he rose near the top of the water and rested, holding on to the chain that secured the buoy to the bottom of the ocean. Letting go, he kicked his fins and pressed his hands tightly to his sides. He purged his regulator and sucked in air from his tank. He swam toward shore, making sure he stayed above thirty feet—he did not want to decompress.

His watch glowed the direction on the compass. Now, arriving on the beach gave him great pleasure. After hiding his diving equipment in his special place under the docks, he went to the nearby pub parking lot. He gazed inside the pub's window, but walked on—skipping the Scotch was a feat, but he ignored the pull to go inside for a drink. Undetected by anyone, he reached his car and drove away from the harbor.

After a short time, he checked into a hotel near Donegal. It was far enough away from Donegal Town so he would not to be recognized, but close enough to drive to the harbor and take a boat back to Blackrock the next night.

He slept badly and woke with a headache. His arms and legs cramped during the night and his dreams woke him. The clock near his bed read 11:00 a.m. He had overslept. Getting up, he stretched and searched the room for the refrigerator.

"Here it is," he said. "Ah—ice cold," he said, taking out two beers. He pressed one to his forehead, the cold felt good—relieved some of the headache. Uncapping it, he drank all of it then started on the next one.

He thought back to his new plan for Laine. Parts of it formed in his mind as he swam underwater the night before.

"So what am I goin' to do with her? Let's see," he said, picking up the notepad and pen next to his phone. He sat on the bed and began writing. "First, go through tunnel to the cave. If she has escaped or if they found her, go to the fireplace hatch. Two, hmmm," he looked at the gray wall in front of him, taking his time. "Yeah, now I have it. Go to her bedroom—take the stairs—through the tower door." He chewed on the pen and tossed the beer down his throat. "Go to her room—the pillow. Yeah, that's it. Suffocate her. Great idea, Jack," he said to himself. "Don't need chloroform this time." He finished the beer and took a shower.

He liked the plan. Pulling his pants and shirt on he thought, they'll never catch a dead man. He laughed. "That's me—dead man."

Studying his unshaven face in the mirror over the desk, he said, "Like it. I look like a paid assassin. Yeah, I'll kill Laine and she'll be payin' me." He laughed harder. "I should be a comedian."

The knock on his door startled him. He wasn't expecting anyone.

He waited—the knock came again.

"Room service," said the maid.

"Come back later," he said in an irritated voice.

Flinging the curtain open, he stared out the window at the small town. People were walking the sidewalks, flanked by flowers, and entering colorful stores along the way. He saw the wood pub sign hanging from a wrought iron post swaying in the breeze.

He thought, "I have to get a boat—but where?" It came to him. He'd take the fisherman's boat that was docked near his curragh in the harbor. He'd never know it was gone—it would be late that evening and dark.

He dropped the key on the unmade bed, towels strewn about on the floor, and walked out the front door of the hotel without paying the room bar bill. Having paid cash and given them an alias when he checked in was a brainstorm. Laughing, he climbed into his car and drove to the end of town where he pulled up in front of the diner.

"Might have Dublin coddle today," he said, and walked inside. He'd go to the pub with the swinging wood sign later while he waited for evening—and Marla. "Oh damn, I almost forgot Marla. Number five on the list, pick up Marla in the cave or in their hiding place on the beach."

He took a booth opposite some men in long white robes. They reminded him of the sheik and Kamal. He got up, went to the bathroom, and left the restaurant without ordering. He drove along the narrow road with mountains on either side of him. They were blue against the brown barren land. In some areas, patches of wildflowers grew in abundance, then the brown land continued. It seemed the mountains closed in on him at times, sharp, hard, rugged and black. Goats stood on ledges, and sheep grazed once he neared the grassy fields. A donkey stuck his face over the fence at one turn, shaking his head with his long ears, up and down. More sheep and dogs littered the road. He swerved to miss a capped old man in a tweed coat, pressing his walking stick into the road, followed by a long-haired black and white dog. The old man's ruddy face peered at him, blue eyes bright, not smiling. He pointed and waved his stick at Jack, other hand fisted. Jack laughed at him and pressed the accelerator to the floor.

In the next town, he found a pub and parked his truck in front of it. It was dark inside when he entered. He liked the dark. It made him feel good. "Scotch," he said. "Got anything to eat?"

The bartender placed a worn menu in front of him. Jack ordered, sipped his drink, and watched television on the wall—killing time.

Down the street, the men in white robes waited, cell phones pressed to their ears.

FORTY-EIGHT
DONEGAL AIRPORT

The same day, the smooth-skinned boy from New Mexico arrived at the Donegal Airport in the long white limousine.

The chauffeur asked him, "Senor Rodriguez, would you like me to get you something to eat while we wait for your father?"

"No, Fredrick, I have eaten." He continued watching his favorite TV series NCIS in the back seat.

The boy's father came to the car.

"Rodriguez," he said in a Spanish accent, embracing his son. "Nice to see you. Your mother sends her love from New Mexico. She is not at the Oklahoma ranch." His brown face was taut and pot-marked, and looked nothing like his son with the smooth brown skin.

"Si, father, I spoke to her this morning. Told her I was waiting for you," said Rodriguez. "Oh," he said, "I like this part." He pointed to the television, watching Mark Harmon sanding his boat on NCIS. "I want to build a boat someday with my own hands."

"Si, and you will Rodriguez." His father smiled and he turned off the television. "Tell me more about your short job—working on Bourke's farm—the horses. Is there more?"

"Si, father, they have the best racehorses—only the finest. I listened carefully. They thought I did not understand them." He had lost his broken English, saying, "I studied hard at the University of Michigan for you father—to help you and our cousin in Mexico with the business. Someday, I will have my own horse business—like you!"

His father nodded, and the gold medallion on the thick linked chain, bounced on his chest. "Si, my son, you will have it soon."

Rodriquez told him the rest. "Father, the horses are the finest—Sheik Abdullah buys them from Bourke. The sheik breeds them at *Koolmoore Stables*—runs them in the most prestigious races in France and the States. I did the 'milkshaking'—I mean—injected the ones that were sold to the sheik—like you told me to do. They did not finish the race—some died. No one saw me."

His father turned his head toward Rodriguez, black eyes wrinkling at the corners. "Ah, yes our competition. Si, you learn quickly. You have done as I have said. Is there more?"

Rodriguez told him about Jack and how he wanted to sell horses to their cousin in Mexico—get involved in the Mexican horseracing business.

"I did not tell him about your horse business, father. Did I do the right thing?" the boy looked at him and waited. He did not tell him about the finder's fee.

"Yes, my son. You made good choices," his father smiled at him. "Go on."

He told him about Rex—the shooting and the hunters, the scaffolding accident. "A man in the bar overheard me make the deal with Jack. He worked for Bourke, so I took care of him. Jack told me what to do—I made it happen, father. I loosened the screws on the scaffolding poles. It failed—the man lived."

"That happens, my son," he said. "That it?"

"No, father. There is more. Bourke is making a party room in his lighthouse on the island. You should see it father. It's going to be used for entertaining people like you—and buyers, I mean." He looked embarrassed.

"Yes, you are right, Rodriguez. I should meet this man Bourke," said his father in a strong voice. "I will arrange it. You are becoming an excellent business man, my son."

"*Gracias,* father."

The father opened his briefcase and took out several packets of one-thousand dollar bills, bound by a thin white piece of paper with red numbers showing the amount. He counted fifty and placed them in a brown sack.

"It serves you well to be a good listener." He handed the sack to Rodriguez.

"Gracias, father, I will invest it wisely—into the horses. Maybe buy from Jack."

"Si," he said. "And in a few years, you will join me in the racehorse business. There are millions to be made—and spent, my son." He pulled a fat cigar from his case, cut the ends off, and lit it. "Here, have one."

His son felt good as he inhaled his first cigar. Today he had become a man in his father's eyes, he thought, smiling, and smoking. "I'll make millions horse racing and horse breeding just like you, father, and my cousin, Jose. This is a good day."

"A very good day. After we reach the hotel, we can go and eat. I am hungry."

"Si, there is a good restaurant in Donegal Bay. Brown trout comes from the sea every day. It's *está deliciosa.* Rice and good wine." Rodriguez smiled. His teeth were no longer stained by the ink he used when he met Jack, but bright, shining, and white.

The father pushed the button to open the glass separating them from the chauffeur. He said, "Fredrick, take us to Donegal to the hotel. We are hungry."

Rodriguez said, "Abbey Hotel in the *Diamond*, the center of Donegal Town."

As soon as they started out on the road away from the airport, newly constructed estates painted yellow and white gave them a fine view. The driver sped along the coast; the ocean was rough, and the wind was blowing the waves away from the shore. Here the country was quite green and punctuated by black rod-iron gates. Statuary surrounded by beds of flowers and overhanging trees were at the end of the long driveways leading to the mansions. Mercedes crowded the entrances.

Later, they rounded a bend and sheep farms blanketed the hillsides. The sheep went along eating the grass. The car flew up a hill and down the next, the farms going on and on, green land rolling over the hills. Rectangular stone hedges, covered in ivy sitting up from the hills, fenced in the sheep. They had a pleasant view of the blue and white striped sheep grazing on the lush green grass.

Now there were only a few indoor and outdoor horse arenas, following one after the other along the road, sporting thoroughbreds and work horses in the barnyards. The view was good and after awhile, a long sandy beach stretched outside the town. Anglers dropped their lines in the green water for saltwater fish. They fished in their wooden curraghs, and the old men were baked brown in the sun. White sails dotted the horizon.

The sun was behind the white clouds that passed over them as they came into Donegal Town. Gray stone pavers whitened by the sun and cracked by the cold winter surrounded the square's sidewalks and made up the streets. A line of people coming from a bus walked through the town square passing the sandstone Statue of the Four Masters.

Rodriguez opened the window and the sea breeze felt cool. "Father, we are here," he said. He sat forward in his seat as the car stopped in front of the Abbey Hotel. He climbed out of the back seat and went into the hotel with his father. He was happy, and that night he would have a good bed to sleep in.

FORTY-NINE
BLACKSOD HARBOR

Later that day, Jack took the fisherman's boat down from his well and arrived on the island around 11:00 p.m. He climbed the path that led him into the dense forest on the far side of the island, away from the lighthouse tower. He dragged himself along another winding path at the top of the black rock cliffs. Waves crashed below along the sandy shores. Merlins slept in their nests inside the crevices of the cliff walls. After stumbling and falling several times, he made it to the tunnel. He crept into the cold dark cave room. Laine was gone. He collapsed on the stone slab, smiling. He would wait for Marla to come back and then he would take care of Laine.

"Damn her," he said. "She's out of luck." He stretched out closing his eyes and rested. After a while, he fell asleep in the cold slab and dreamt of lions roaming the fields.

FIFTY

BLACKROCK ISLAND

Laine walked to her room and closed the door. She placed a call on her cell phone. "Max, I think I know what's going on."

"Okay, let's have it," he said. "I'm recording this."

"Good," she said. "It started when I went to Ireland, and I thought I saw John in the square. I did and he saw me."

"Go on, Laine," he said in a hard voice.

"Next, the hunters shot Miles' horse Rex on his farm. The horse needed to be replaced. A man called Jack Rafferty bought one of Miles' horses at the Donegal Auction—a look-a-like for Rex, but no one put that together, until now. He was buying the horse and was going to pass him off as Rex. He thought the sheik didn't know about the shooting and was going to make a few bucks off the horse resembling Rex. But unknown to him, the sheik did know and he had already replaced the horse with two new Arabian horses. Miles and the sheik cut a deal without the broker, and the sheik found out he paid an extra million for Rex that he didn't know about, plus Jack's commission. We also found out Jack skimmed more than a million off the top for himself by overcharging the sheik. This was no coincidence."

"I'm getting it," said Max.

"This got me thinking. How is "Jack" connected to everything?"

"Something stinks," said Miles in a hard voice.

Laine said, "You're right about that." She checked her notes.

"What else do you have?"

"There was an accident—but it wasn't an accident. It was intentional when Murray got hurt on the Miles' construction sight. We pieced the information together based on a conversation Murray overhead in a bar the night Eamon was hiring people for odd jobs. A man, Jack, hired a Mexican boy to steal my schedule and to listen to everything that was going on at the farm and on the island. He also made a deal with the boy to sell horses to his cousin in Mexico. The Mexican boy would get a finder fee for each horse his Mexican cousin bought. Jack told the boy he was interested in doing business and to keep it to himself. This was all supposed to be a secret, but Murray overheard it. When the boy found out Murray knew, he or Jack tried to kill him on the construction site. Why again, I asked myself?"

"Follow the money," said Max.

"Then it came to me, after I saw the Mexican boy and Jack exchange money on the docks on the island. The man looked familiar. It was hard to tell from a distance, but it got me thinking. What if Jack is John?" She stopped, and remembered it.

"Laine?" he said in a low tone.

"I'm fine," she said in a hard voice. "Now I know it was John. He was Jack and he was alive. He and his girlfriend, Marla, tried to kill me. You know how that turned out. Well, I pieced the rest of it together, after I got over the shock. John died in a boating accident not far from the island, after he tried to kill me, and Marla blew up in Miles' helicopter. That's what we have. You can figure out the rest."

"Let me try helping you," said Max. "Given what you told me, John would inherit your money and the land in Ireland, if you were dead. He was skimming off the top with the sheik and who knows how many more suckers. Easy to launder money on his end, because he was the middleman—no one to keep track. Shamus found out some details at Carrick's Pub thanks to your intel.

We also discovered Jack was helping the Mexican cartel in Michigan. He was moving drugs from Detroit into Canada by using wave runners and older people as dealers in the South Channel. He was not directly involved in the 'milkshaking' incidents. That was the Mexican boy, but he was supplying drug runners in Detroit to funnel the dope to the rest of the US."

"That's what I thought," said Laine. "I knew the boat was in the area of Squirrel Island for some reason. He rammed the boat on the rocks and walked into Canada. Makes sense.

Miles said, "The Mexican boy Rodriguez was a different story altogether."

"Yes," she said. "He and Jack hooked up in Ireland. It was a perfect fit. The boy had international connections with his cousin in Mexico. But I discovered a new clue. I thought, what if the Mexican boy was not from Mexico like his cousin, but lived in New Mexico? Jack and the boy could have been involved in tampering with the horses—using the drugs for the 'milkshaking' in Kentucky and in France. It got me thinking. I knew it."

"You got it. The Mexican cartel. The kid's the son of Juan Diez, head of the Mexican cartel—the Don. I knew I had heard that name before. Hold the phone—better yet, I'll call you back. I have to contact the DEA and our agents to get them up to speed. Good job. I'll call you later with an update." He hung up.

Laine stared at the phone. She was not finished. John was selling drugs in Detroit and using her. How could she have missed it? She was so wrapped up in her own work that she didn't even notice. The signs were there. Let it go, she told herself. He can't hurt you anymore. The operation in Ireland was over on her end, but it was only beginning for the other operatives.

She walked to the window and watched the waves roll over and over in the Atlantic. The warm breeze felt good as she took in the fine view. She would finish her job designing the party room in the lighthouse for Miles. A party room for racehorse owners, breeders, and buyers—a good room with plenty of light. It was time to get back to work. She left the bedroom and went up the winding staircase to the map room. The sun was shining through the new window. The room was warm, and she felt good.

"I'm free," she thought.

The Atlantic looked different—like she never saw it before. The black rock cliffs jutted up into the cloudless blue sky, and the sun shined on the water. The light danced, flickered, and skipped along the crests of the waves—sharp white light on the surface. She heard the warbling of skylarks—not the ravens, and the peregrine falcons. It was a cacophony of sounds mingling with the warm sea breeze. A Gavia immer (Great Northern Diver), with its heavy spear-like bill, circled above the green foamy waves, gliding low on the water. On the edge of the black rock cliffs, even the trees in the forest looked greener—more alive.

"Laine, everything all right?" said Miles, entering the map room.

"Yes, Miles, it's perfect," she said. "Let's have a party."

FIFTY-ONE

Later that night while Laine and Miles were celebrating, men in long white robes moved silently into the cave where Jack was sleeping. The lead turbaned man covered Jack's mouth with his hand, and another quickly slit his throat from ear to ear. They placed him in a black bag and zipped it up. Another man slung him over his shoulder and carried him out of the cave. Taking the path through the forest to the back of the island was easy going. They had marked the trail to the boat they had pulled up on the shore. Pushing off from the rocky land, they headed out to sea.

When the boat reached the halfway point in the deepest part of the ocean, they unzipped the bag and dumped the body overboard. It floated for a moment, bobbing up and down in the waves. They watched and waited under the full moon.

Gray pointed fins broke the surface of the water, the fish swimming fast and smooth, in a direct line to the body. Several sharks circled the floating man. A frenzied dance began. Striking, ripping, and tearing the flesh, they fought over the pieces. In a short time, the water bubbled with dark red blood and dissipated in the sea. Soon the sharks moved away. There was no more blood in the water. Finished with their job, the men put the boat in gear and sped toward the harbor.

FIFTY-TWO

After Miles' helicopter exploded, the wreckage was carted off the island, and the police and the peacekeepers left the area. The clean-up was quick, and what was left of the disaster was the black, scorched earth where the helicopter had exploded.

Miles said, "Laine, let's go to Donegal and take some time off today. We can stop by Margaret Hogan's office and look up your deed. Then we can have lunch. What do you think?"

The sun streamed through the kitchen window. They stood, looking at each other.

"Yes, Miles, I'd like that. It's a good idea." She started to sip her tea, but changed her mind.

"The Trumpy is all set to go." He set his cup in the sink.

"The boat. Yes, I'd like to go by boat." She squeezed his hand. "Guess you have to get a new helicopter."

"Something I do often," he laughed, his voice warm. "I'll meet you there in fifteen?" He kissed her.

"I liked that," she said.

"Sure."

"Oh, Miles, we could have a good time."

"We don't have to leave, if you don't want to."

"It would be better."

"Only if you want to."

"Yes, I want to."

He turned his head and looked at her. "There'll be other days."

"Yes. Let's go and eat. Have a good time."

"Sure." She picked up her teacup and emptied it in the sink "I think I'll start drinking the black tea Patricia has been giving me. I've had enough of this." She threw her favorite tea tin in the trash.

They left the cottage and headed down the stone steps to Miles' boat. The crew casted off, and they cruised to Donegal. The breeze was warm on the stern, and they sat sipping iced tea, looking at the horizon.

"I feel good," Laine said.

"It is a good day."

"Yes. It's over."

"I've been meaning to ask you something," he said.

"Not sure if I'll answer." Laine laughed, watching the wake curl off each side at the back of the boat. She sat next to him on the couch in the rose wood cabin.

"It's about the gun," he said.

"It's nothing." She felt her face muscles tighten and knew he was watching her.

"Yes, it's nothing," he said in a quiet voice.

"You asked me that before. That one day, you asked me with your eyes."

"Yes."

"So we won't talk of it. Never."

"No, we won't. Never."

Laine leaned over and kissed him. "I like you, Miles. You're a good man."

"Sure," he said smiling, and threw his arm around her shoulder. "Feels right. I think we should go to Cong. Visit Ashford Castle and fish for brown trout. I'll hire a guile (guide). We can go out on the water in the early morning and take a curragh, before it gets warm on Lough Corrib."

"Yes, I'd like that."

"That's what we'll do tomorrow. Fish. Fish on Lough Corrib."

"We'll have a good time."

"Yes, we will have a good time. My ancestors built the castle on a beautiful piece of land on the Cong River. It is a good place."

"Lovely, we will have a good time."

"Sure," he smiled at her. "You'll be alright."

"Yes," she said. "I am."

They cruised to Donegal Harbor under the bright sunlight.

FIFTY-THREE
MARGARET HOGAN'S REAL ESTATE OFFICE

Before noon, Miles and Laine pulled into Donegal Harbor on his yacht.

Miles said, "The flag is flying half-staff on the *Morrigan*. Looks like no one is on board the waterbus.

"I see that. Wonder why."

They walked the short distance to Margaret Hogan's real estate office.

"Afternoon, Margaret," said Miles as they entered.

"Good afternoon to you, and Laine, she said rising from her desk. "Won't you have a seat?"

"Yes," said Laine. "Good to see you again."

Miles said, "Saw the flag half-staff on the *Morrigan*. Who died?"

"Captain's wife, Marla. We heard today," she said. "'Tis no loss."

"What do you mean his wife?" said Miles.

"I'll not be mournin' the likes of Marla. Didn't you know she married the captain of the *Morrigan* 'bout a year ago?"

"No," said Miles, "news to me."

"Laine said, "Marla? John's Marla?"

"Don't know about no John. Carryin' on with some Jack fella she was. 'Twas a blessing for the captain to be rid of her. They was sayin' she met her end in a bad way, they did." She sat at her desk, flipping papers. "Not sure what it was about. All the fuss and that."

Miles was silent.

Laine said nothing, wondering how she had missed it. Marla was in the helicopter when it exploded. She would update Max. Marla was part of Jack's scheme to kill her.

"Well, then, sorry for the captain," Miles said clearing his throat. "On a happier note, you mentioned you have the deed for the Sullivan property?"

"I've gone and found the deed, but there's a bit of a problem. *I* can't be givin' it to you, Laine."

"That's alright," said Laine. "It wasn't really mine to have."

"Aye, it is, lass, but it is."

"I'm confused. I thought you said I can't have it."

"Alright then, I did," she smiled and shouted to the back room. "Bring the deed out here, will you, Norbert?"

Norbert, a white-haired man of several years entered the office. He was smiling. His cheeks were red, and his eyes were blue and bright. "Here it is, Margaret. Miles, it is good to see you again. You must be Laine."

Laine stared at him. She could not speak. She was taken aback by the looks of him.

Miles stood up. "Norbert, so glad to see you," said Miles, pumping his hand.

Laine said, "My God, it can't be. You look exactly like my father."

"That I do," he said. "Laine, this may come as a shock, but I'm your father's brother, I am."

"Brother." She stood up from the chair.

"His twin brother, that is. Had a fallin' out when we was young. "

"This is crazy," Laine said in an anxious voice.

"Aye, I'll be needin' to make up for not telling you sooner. You're all I have left of family, Laine. The rest is gone."

"Norbert," she said. "I am so happy to meet you." She threw her arms around him, hugging him to her. Pushing away, she studied his face. "I can't believe it. My father's twin brother." She clutched at his arms, examining his face.

Miles said, "Margaret told us you went to Michigan. Then we heard you had disappeared."

"Aye, but not in the sense you're thinking of. I couldn't remember who I was for quite some time. There was an accident," Norbert said.

"What happened?" Laine said.

"It may be a bit hard on you, if I tell you, lass," Norbert said.

"I'd like to hear it," said Laine in a hard tone.

"I almost drowned."

"What do you mean?" Laine was feeling bad. "Drowned?"

"I was in Michigan with your husband John—sailing in the South Channel off Lake St. Clair," he said in a soft voice. "It wasn't in me plans, but that's what happened."

"John?"

"Aye, I was with your husband. He tried to kill me."

"What are you talking about?"

Norbert told them the story of his near drowning, the amnesia, and his rescue by the Gudefin's—the French-Canadian couple living in their summer home near Squirrel Island.

"This is shocking," Laine said in a sad voice.

"Aye, there's more. I went to your Grosse Pointe home, Laine. I wanted to give you the deed to me property in person. Surprise you," he said in a low tone. "John told me you were out of town. 'Tis a bad sort that husband of yours, Laine. Hope you know it." He pushed his hands through his white hair, smoothing it back. "Really bad he is."

"Yes, I know."

Norbert said in an angry tone, "He said you were in New York workin'. Invited me to go sailin' with him that very day I was at your home. Told him I couldn't swim, I did. Convinced me it was no matter. Like a fool, I went with him."

Margaret said, "Yes, I was worried sick for months after you didn't come home or call. I'll be remembering it for a while now, I will." Margaret gave him a look.

"Oh, Margaret, let me tell the lass the story," he said smiling at her.

"Go on then," she said.

"I got knocked in me head by the boat beam when we gibed—tossed me overboard, it did. I was callin' John for help, but it make no difference to him—he didn't come back for me. I watched him sailed away. Left me in the water hangin' on to the sail and part of the riggin'."

"I am so sorry," Laine said. "He's an evil man. I feel responsible."

"It's not your fault, Laine," said Norbert. "It's in him—the evil. It's not in you, lass."

Miles said, "John can't hurt anyone anymore. He's dead, Norbert. He drowned yesterday at sea. The police found his currah—empty—out by the Olympic buoys."

Margaret said and blessed herself, "I'll not be mornin' the likes of him."

No one said anything for a few minutes.

"Well, here we are, Laine." Norbert took her hand in his.

"It feels good to know I have family," Laine said.

"Aye, that it does," Norbert said.

"So glad you're back on Irish soil," said Miles to Norbert.

"I'll be forgivin' you, Norbert, but you best be watchin' your step in the future."

"That I will," said Norbert going around behind the desk, giving Margaret a hug.

"Yes," said Laine. "It means a lot to me."

Norbert smiled. "Don't be worried. Laine, I have something for you." He reached into the breast pocket of his coat. "Here this is for you. It's the deed to the Sullivan property—the original deed. Don't forget you're a Sullivan, lass."

"I am overwhelmed. Thank you, and I won't forget."

"Good to know," he said. "Anyone tell you that you look like your mum?"

She nodded and smiled at him. "I'm a lot like her. And my father."

"That I'll have to be seein' for myself," Norbert said.

"Let's celebrate this happy occasion," said Miles. "I'm buying."

"Come on, Norbert and Margaret," said Laine. "I'm going to order a martini."

"Sounds good to me," said Norbert. "Comin', Margaret?"

"I am," she followed them out of the office, locking the door behind them.

FIFTY-FOUR
LOUGH CORRIB AND THE RIVER CONG

They ate a fine meal at Donahue's Pub. Later, they walked along the docks in the sunset. Laine was happy and she knew they were good people. Maybe this time it would be different. Margaret and Norbert left them after a short time.

Miles said, "Don't forget. We're going fishing tomorrow."

"Sure," Laine said. "Bet you the biggest fish."

"You're on."

He took her hand, and they walked down to the harbor beach area. The sand felt good on their feet. The water was clear and the sun was a warm orange glow on the horizon.

"To fishing," said Miles.

"And—to the catch and release," said Laine in a happy voice, "on Lough Corrib and the River Cong." She watched the sunset. It shut out the darkness.

ENDORSEMENT

You will enjoy and possibly reread a page or two as you will not want to miss a syllable. Mystery, romance, bewilderment, history and more fill this book from first time author Judy Burke. The author knows, shares and creates. Here is to her next book.

—Geraldine Hempel Davis

Geraldine Hempel Davis worked for the J.Walter Thompson advertising agency, was the youngest woman on the production team of The Ed Sullivan Show, and was for several years a contributing correspondent for The Today Show. She is the author of the authorized history of The Today Show as well as The Moving Experience. She lives in Virginia.

CPSIA information can be obtained at www.ICGtesting.com
Printed in the USA
LVOW06s0438141114

413646LV00002B/467/P